THE ADVENTURE G

AT HAPPINESS HOUSE

By

Clair Blank

Chapter I

BRIARHURST

With a final chug and screech of brakes the train slid to a halt before the two story frame building that did duty for a railway station in the little college town of Briarhurst.

A group of girls proceeded with much hilarity and little speed to transport themselves and their luggage from the railway coach to the station platform. From there they viewed the rusty bus that was to transport them up the hill to the college grounds.

"It will never hold all of us and our luggage," Carol Carter declared with firm conviction. "Perhaps we had better walk."

Janet Gordon looked at the dusty road winding up the hill behind the station and then at the bus. "You can walk," she said. "I'll take a chance on this antiquated vehicle."

"Are you the six young ladies goin' to Briarhurst?"

The girls turned to see a wizened old man approaching from the station. "If ye are, climb aboard. I'm the bus driver."

"I'll wager the bus is even older than he is," Madge Reynolds murmured to Valerie Wallace.

"Will the contraption hold together?" Carol wanted to know.

"It's been a-runnin' for nigh onto twenty years and ain't fell apart yet," the driver said, climbing into his seat and waiting for the girls to get aboard.

"That isn't saying it never will," Phyllis Elton commented.

After much dickering the girls got into the bus, their luggage for the most part piled on the roof, and the ancient vehicle with its ancient driver started with a roar.

"It reminds me of a peanut roaster," Carol murmured. "The way the radiator is steaming and the noise it makes."

"Everything but the peanuts," agreed Janet. "Which reminds me, I hope dinner is early."

"Dinner is at seven," the driver informed them conversationally.

The bus started the long tedious climb up the hillside and the driver settled back comfortably in his seat. He was in no hurry.

"I thought Briarhurst was a prosperous college," Phyllis Elton said to Gale Howard, "wouldn't you think they would have a more modern bus? This thing might scare new students."

The driver frowned on her with all the disgust possible to his wrinkled features.

"Lizzie, here, has belonged to the college since she was new. She's good enough for you yet. Even the new Dean can't junk old Lizzie." He patted the steering wheel with all the affection and prized possessiveness of a loving father.

"New Dean?" Gale questioned. "Isn't Professor Harris the Dean any more?"

"Nope," the driver said. "Professor Harris resigned an' this new one come up here about three weeks ago. She's been tryin' to make changes we old ones don't like."

The girls exchanged glances. They had heard so much about Professor Harris and her rule at Briarhurst. The Dean had been much beloved by the girls. The prospect of a new régime at the college did not particularly appeal to them.

"What's she like—the new Dean?" Janet asked interestedly.

"Young and purty," the sour old man said grudgingly. "But she got no business tryin' to change things that been goin' on all right for thirty years. She won't stay long," he added darkly.

"Why won't she stay?" Phyllis wanted to know.

"The old ones don't like her," he said firmly.

"By 'the old ones' I take it you mean the teachers and other members of the faculty," Gale said.

"That's right," he agreed.

"What has she done to make them dislike her?" Janet inquired.

The man shook his head. "We don't aim to make this a modern institooshun. She has newfangled notions about a new bus and sports for the young ladies. We old ones ain't goin' to stand for it," he repeated firmly. Evidently he considered himself an important part of the college personnel.

"The idea about a new bus is enough to prejudice him," Carol laughed to Janet. "Whoops!" She made a wild lunge for her handbag as the bus navigated a deep rut with a series of protesting groans from the framework. "However, it is enough to put me on her side. If she wants a new bus I am for the new Dean!"

The bus halted first in front of the registrar's office and the girls were assigned to their prospective quarters. Because of crowded conditions only Phyllis and Gale were fortunate enough to win a room in the sorority house of Omega Chi, and this was only through the efforts of their former High School teacher. The other four girls were assigned to the dormitory house on the east lawn of the campus. At first the separation rather put a damper on their spirits.

"You might get into the sorority house next year," consoled Phyllis.

"As it is," Janet commented, "we will leave you two to face the dragons of the sorority by yourselves."

The next stop of the bus was to let Gale and Phyllis off in front of the Omega Chi Sorority house. They surveyed their future home interestedly while standing in the midst of their baggage which the driver had dumped unceremoniously at their feet. The bus rattled away and the girls exchanged glances.

"We might as well go in," Phyllis said finally.

Several girls were on the veranda and these viewed with interest the new arrivals.

"We might as well," Gale agreed with a sigh. With a traveling bag in either hand she followed Phyllis up the steps and into the building that was to be their home for the next four years.

Chapter II

A RESCUE

"I am not going to like it!" Janet announced firmly when she met Phyllis and Gale on the campus the next morning after breakfast.

"You are lucky so far," Phyllis told her. "The upper classmen in the dormitories haven't come back for the term yet. We have some of the sorority girls already in the house and do we get looked over!"

"Where is Carol?" Gale inquired.

"Gone to get our tennis racquets," Janet replied. "We are going to take advantage of the empty courts now before the upper classmen get here."

"I'll come along and watch," Phyllis offered magnanimously.

"I want to take a walk and explore," Gale informed them. "I'll see you at luncheon, Phyl."

Classes would not begin for three days yet, but the girls had timed their arrival at Briarhurst for days ahead to become acquainted with the general position of their classes and the dormitories.

Gale headed in the direction of the lake that lay on the western border of the campus. There had been erected diving boards for the students and canoes were anchored to the shore. Gale watched for several minutes the cavortings of the gay young girls who frolicked in the water, and then continued with her stroll.

Readers of The Adventure Girls at K Bar O and The Adventure Girls in the Air are already familiar with the six girls from the little town of Marchton. Old friends already know of the desire of the girls to attend Briarhurst College and of the difficulties along that line experienced by Phyllis Elton. Now it seemed their dreams were in a fair way of being fulfilled. All of them, even Phyllis, were actually present at the college and starting out on an entirely new branch of life. They were prepared to study hard and also prepared to face the fun and trials of college life.

On the grassy bank beneath a low-hanging willow tree Gale sat down to view the water and to think.

Last night they had been met at the door by a welcoming committee of two Juniors. She remembered her own and Phyllis' surprise at the odd things which they saw on their journey to their room on the third floor.

Some delightful soul had christened the staircase the "Golden Stairs," but whether they led to heaven or not the girls had not yet discovered. On the landing of the second floor was a huge poster which might have been the street sign for a Boulevard proclaiming "Senior Avenue." On each floor the corridor was named and some of the rooms themselves had names.

Phyllis and Gale found themselves in "Sunshine Alley" but there was no name tacked upon their door.

"How come?" Phyllis wanted to know.

"You have to do something to deserve a name. Then a special committee of sorority girls gets together and selects one for you. For instance, next door to you, you have the champion swimming team of last year's Freshman class. Their room is named 'Mermaid Mansion.' Get the idea?"

"Also farther up the hall is 'Harmony Heaven,'" the other upper classman informed them. "That was so named because the girls there are forever quarreling. The name anything but fits them."

It was a little confusing to Gale and Phyllis. They could not immediately adapt the terms for the different floors and rooms in the house. At dinner when someone asked them what floor they were on, they innocently said "Third," and were made to run around the table three times for not using the correct title "Sunshine Alley."

For the most part, though, the girls were friendly. The two were shown about with due ceremony and the rules carefully explained. The house mother, Mrs. Grayson, who had charge of the building was most courteous and the girls immediately liked her. Next they met the sorority president, Adele Stevens. They were at once taken under her wing.

Gale dangled the end of a willow branch in the swirling lake water. The water at this point was flowing rapidly toward a waterfall where it joined a rushing river and went on to the sea.

This afternoon she had an appointment with the President of the college and then one with the Dean. It was customary for all new students to be thus interviewed, but Gale wondered if they all felt as nervous as she. She had a strong curiosity and yet a reluctance to meet the new Dean. She wanted to see the new authority because the girls had talked about her so much at dinner last night. It seemed the Seniors all sympathized with the bus driver. They were prepared to strongly oppose any new policies installed by Dean Travis. From what Gale and Phyllis had heard, the new Dean's policies would better things on the campus. At least they appealed favorably to the new Freshmen. Certainly there could be nothing wrong in wanting new laboratories for the Chemistry classes, a new organ for the chapel, stables and horses to teach the girls riding and a few other such things. Why the older students were so set against them Phyllis and Gale could not understand. However, they both agreed, in the privacy of their room, to take neither side until they knew more about things. At any rate, they were only Freshmen and Freshmen were to be seen, not heard.

Gale was about to turn back to the campus to meet Phyllis for luncheon at the sorority house when she halted. Had that been a voice calling? Faintly another call came across the water. Parting the low thick branches of the willow tree, Gale looked across the lake.

A canoe was drifting down the center of the lake. It was going more swiftly every moment, caught in the rush of waters leaping on toward the waterfall at the other end. In the canoe was a figure, waving frantically to the shore.

Either the canoeist had lost her oars or she was so panic-stricken at being caught in the swirling waters that she could not think conclusively or quickly enough to save herself.

A tree branch had been broken from a tree in a recent storm and now it, too, swirled around in the lake waters. Gale watched breathlessly while the branch bore down on the canoe. She was helpless to aid even though the onslaught would probably upset the canoe. But such was not the case. Instead of toppling the canoe over the boat became entangled in the wet leaves still clinging to the wood and so, locked together, the two moved toward the waterfall.

Gale started to run swiftly back to where, in the calmer waters, the college girls had been swimming. Someone must rescue that woman in the canoe. Perhaps there would be a motor boat at the diving boards. Another canoe would not be much help. Gale kept close to the shore as she ran, always keeping in view of the canoe. Once she stopped to wave to the tragic figure being swept to destruction. She saw an answering wave and heard a call, but she could not distinguish the words.

Fortunately she did not have to run all the way back to the swimmers. Hidden close to the mossy bank in a thick growth of shrubbery along the shore was a motor boat. Gale found it with a sense of immeasurable relief. With trembling fingers she untied the anchor rope and jumped into the boat. How thankful she was that she had had ample experience with motor boats back in Marchton! It stood her in good stead now. The motor responded promptly and she turned the nose of the boat out into the lake. She drew speed from the boat and wondered what the owner might say.

The canoe, still tangled with the dead tree branch, was even closer to the tumbling waters going over the waterfall. Gale was glad the motor boat was a large, sturdy affair. With its powerful motor working rhythmically it should be able to withstand the pull of those rushing waters.

Flinging a heavy spray back over Gale the boat sped eagerly through the water. It rapidly closed the distance between the drifting canoe and the would-be rescuer. Almost upon the canoe Gale tried to think of the best means of getting the woman safely aboard the motor boat. She certainly could not be transferred from the canoe in the middle of the water. Therefore, the best procedure would be to tow the canoe to shore. But first the tree branch must be disposed of. It might drag both the canoe and the motor boat to the falls.

"Hang on," Gale shouted to the figure in the canoe, "we'll make the shore all right."

She ran the motor boat as close as she could to the canoe. The swell of water threatened to upset the smaller craft. Gale shut the motor off. The boat was immediately swept into the current. Grasping a long, heavy boat hook which she found lying on the deck, Gale stepped onto the closed cabinet-like doors which sheltered the engine.

"Go back—you'll be killed!" the other figure implored.

Gale sent the woman a reassuring smile. She had done such crazy stunts on Bruce Latimer's boat back in Marchton. Now she felt no fear at all for herself, only a fear that she might not be able to push the tree branch far enough away to loosen the canoe. She tied one end of a coil of rope to the anchor bolt on the motor boat and threw it toward the canoe. It fell directly across the small craft. The canoeist grasped it and made it secure.

Cautiously Gale worked herself farther out to the bow of the boat. She had only a few seconds now in which to loosen the tree branch and restart the motor to save them both. At the first thrust of the boat hook Gale nearly toppled herself into the water. She heard a muffled cry from the woman in the canoe. She regained her posture. She could never do it standing upright. Therefore, she lay down flat on her stomach on the boat. That gave her a freer use of her right arm and less chance of losing her balance. A gigantic push and the branch swept away from the canoe and onward to the destruction of the falls.

Gale lost no time in making her way back to start the motor. Luckily it started with the first try and the motor boat pulled clear of the swirling waters, dragging behind it the canoe.

Once on shore Gale tied the motor boat securely to its former position and helped the slender figure from the canoe. The canoeist was a woman older than Gale, but Gale felt immediately that they could be firm friends. She liked the other's frank smile and clear gray eyes.

"You are a brave girl!" the woman said when she was safe and her first words of thanks were over. "I might be over the falls now if it were not for you," she shuddered.

Gale smiled. "It was a lucky thing someone was here. What happened? Did you go out without any oars?"

"I know better than to do that," the woman said. "I was sitting in the canoe farther up along the shore, reading. I often do that. I had no desire to go out on the lake so I left the oars on shore while the boat remained anchored. I must have fallen asleep. The next thing I knew I awoke and I was in the middle of the lake, caught in the rapids."

Gale looked at the boat and noted the short bit of rope dangling from its stern.

"It rather looks as though that rope was cut," she said, noting the sharpness of its edge as though a knife had severed it.

"You must never mention that to anyone," the other said quickly. "Promise me you will never speak such a thought!"

Gale laughed. "Of course—but why shouldn't I?"

"I can't explain now, but there is a very good reason." She held out her hand. "I would like to say thank you again. Will you come to see me this afternoon?"

Gale put her hand into the one offered her. "I'm sorry," she said regretfully. "You see I am new at the college and I have an appointment with the Dean."

A whimsical light came into the gray eyes. "You don't seem very enthusiastic."

"I'm not," Gale confessed.

"Have you been listening to the upper classmen?"

"A little," Gale said. "But it isn't that. I'm not prejudiced against her. She may be perfectly all right—it is only that—I'm a little nervous. I guess all Freshmen are. I hope she is nicer than what I hear about her."

The other woman laughed. "I hope you find her so. Now I——"

The patter of running feet interrupted her and a group of girls burst upon them.

"We saw what happened from up the shore," one gasped. "Are you all right, Dean Travis?"

Dean Travis! Gale felt the world whirling around her. This was the new Dean!

"I am quite all right, thank you," the Dean was saying composedly.

A second later she was gone and the other girls with her. Gale was alone and she sank down dejectedly on a tree trunk. For a long time she sat there staring out over the water. Finally she made her way slowly back to the sorority house where Phyllis was waiting for her.

That afternoon Gale went to the office of the Dean. If she had been nervous this morning before she met the Dean she was ten times more so now. To think of the things she had said! They made her cheeks burn now. How could she have talked so and to the Dean! She sat on the hard outer office chair and thought of all the places she would rather be. She thought of Phyllis and Madge and Valerie swimming in the lake. She thought of Janet and Carol again playing tennis. How she longed to be with them. How she longed to be anywhere where she did not have to face the Dean!

"You may go in, Miss Howard," the secretary said.

Gale stood up and took a deep breath. She covered the distance into the office in little less than a run. She felt she had to go as quickly as possible before she turned and fled out of sheer panic.

There was another woman with Dean Travis, a woman with brown curly hair and a flashing, whimsical smile, absurdly young to be the school physician, but such Gale found her to be when they were introduced. She stayed to talk with Gale and the Dean for several minutes and the Freshman felt all her self-consciousness and timidity melting away before the warmth of the Doctor's smile. However, when the Doctor had gone and the Dean was seated behind her desk, Gale in the chair before her, the girl felt her discomfiture returning. After all, this woman was the Dean and she had talked to her and treated her much as she might have Phyllis or Valerie. Hereafter she must remember to treat the Dean with the respect and deference required by the head of the girls' college.

"Is your room at the Omega Chi Sorority house satisfactory?" the Dean was asking pleasantly. She tapped a white envelope before her. "I have had a long letter from your former High School teacher, Miss Relso."

"Everything is perfect, thank you," Gale said politely.

"Your roommate is your friend from home?"

"Oh, yes."

"I hope you are going to like Briarhurst, Miss Howard."

"I am sure I shall."

"The girls are all pleasant, that is for the most part. Of course there are some who are selfish and like their own way, but one finds them in every walk of life. Briarhurst tries to fit the girls to take a definite place in the world, to help them live the kind of life worth living. We don't say we fit you to immediately take charge of whatever line of endeavor you go into when your four years here are up. All we try to do is give you the prime essentials for your life—courage, determination, ambition, the desire to play fair and to take gallantly whatever life offers you." She smiled. "What is the matter, Gale?"

"Matter?" Gale was surprised out of her respectful silence.

"You have been sitting there politely listening, but I doubt if a word I've said has remained in your memory," the Dean said humorously.

"Oh, I assure you, it has," Gale said hastily.

"Are you still nervous about meeting—the Dean?" the older woman asked, rising and walking around the desk to Gale's side.

Gale also rose. "I'm sorry if I was rude this morning," she said in embarrassment. "I had no idea——"

"That I was the Dean?" the other said. "Otherwise you would have let the canoe drift over the falls, is that it? I'm sorry, that was a terrible thing to say," she continued breathlessly. "Forgive me." She laid a hand lightly on Gale's shoulder. "This isn't the type of interview I usually have with a Freshman."

"I gathered that much," Gale smiled. She continued after a while, rather hesitantly, "You aren't really worried about—about the things the girls are saying, are you?"

"No," the Dean smiled, walking to the door with Gale. "Not really worried. Goodbye, my dear, and come to see me often—as a friend, if not in my official capacity."

Gale stepped out into the world red with the glow from the setting sun and thought what a grand person Dean Travis was. She had a personality that made one immediately want to be the best sort of person one could. That she would in a short time win all the girls over to her side, Gale did not doubt. She was so pleasant, so easy to approach, so interested in the girls, that they could not resent her for any length of time no matter how much they missed their former Dean.

A hand touched her arm and she jumped in surprise, so deep in thought had she been.

"Did I frighten you?" a laughing voice asked.

Doctor Norcot fell into step beside her. "I waited for you," she added with a look around.

Gale saw a few girls across the campus watching her and the Doctor. She hoped they weren't the Adventure Girls. If such was the case, she would be teased intolerably about already being friends with two such important people as the Dean and the Doctor.

"I wanted to ask you more about that cut rope."

"Cut rope?" Gale repeated, puzzled. "Oh, you mean on the canoe."

"Yes. Are you positive it was cut?"

Gale nodded. "There couldn't be any doubt about it. You see it was just a new rope. That is, the end that was left was new. It couldn't have worn through. The edge was straight and not at all frayed. It had been cut," she said firmly. "Did Dean Travis tell you about it?"

"Yes. You haven't told anyone, have you?"

"No," Gale said in mystification. "But why shouldn't I? Anyone who looks at the canoe will be sure to see it."

"Freshmen have enough on their minds without adding other people's troubles," the Doctor teased. "Good afternoon, Miss Howard."

Eyes grown stormy with indignation and then calmer with humor, Gale watched her stride across the campus and into the red brick building which housed the infirmary and the Doctor's quarters.

"What a nice, polite way of telling me to mind my own business," she laughed to herself. "But just the same," she added mischievously, "I won't mind it. I, too, would like to know why that rope was cut so Dean Travis' canoe would drift out and be caught in the rapids."

She walked across the campus toward the sorority house. The building was gray and ivy covered. The sun's last rays made the vine leaves gleam silver and gold in turn. "Happiness House!" She smiled. What a fitting name for the place. Whoever had substituted such a name for the intimate use of the girls had chosen it rightly enough. There seemed to be nothing but peace, contentment and utter harmony among the girls. At least so far she and Phyllis had discovered nothing else. Of course when the rest of the girls arrived for the semester things might be different.

She mounted the steps and entered the living room. There were several girls there, gathered about the piano. One held a ukulele and as Gale went toward the staircase she started to sing:

"There was a happy young Freshman,
Who rescued the Dean from the water,
But alas and alack, now the Freshman is sad,
Cause she did something she hadn't oughter."

Gale laughed and ran lightly up the Golden Stairs to Sunshine Alley. The rhyming was decidedly bad in the girl's song.

Just as she reached the door to her room the most blood-curdling yell came through the panels that she had to pause and put her hands over her ears. From all along the hall doors opened and heads were poked out.

Gale turned the door knob and entered. Phyllis was sitting on the bed convulsed with laughter. Astride the footboard of her bed was another girl, evidently the one who had given voice to that shout because her mouth was still open.

"What on earth——" Gale began.

"My roommate," Phyllis managed to gasp between giggles.

"Howdy!" The girl who was using the bed footboard as a horse said, extending a brown hand. "I'm Ricky Allen. I'm in the room across the hall."

"I'm glad to know you," Gale said, laughing in spite of herself, "but would you mind telling me what that noise was just now?"

Phyllis wiped the tears from her eyes. "Ricky is from Wyoming and she was illustrating a cowboy round-up whoop for me."

There was a heavy knock upon the door. Gale opened it.

"Who is being murdered?" Adele Stevens asked calmly.

Gale shook her head. "It was a mistake. It seems only a cowboy war-whoop got loose. We have it under control now," she added.

When the Sorority president was gone Ricky grinned at the two girls.

"Reckon I'm goin' to like this place now I've met you. I didn't at first. I was lonesome for my ranch and my horses."

"I understand the new Dean plans to have stables and horses installed to teach the girls riding," Gale said.

"Yipeeee!" Ricky greeted the news eagerly. "That'll be great. I've gotta tell my roommate that!"

She was gone with the same suddenness and whirlwind speed that characterized all her actions. Gale and Phyllis looked at one another and burst out laughing.

Chapter III

BELL NIGHT

Classes started and with them the Freshmen's troubles. New acquaintances, new scenes, new studies, and new instructors came with such rapidity that the girls were dizzy with it all. Carol and Janet were in the same dormitory building as Valerie and Madge. Consequently their close friendship was by no means interrupted. Gale and Phyllis went to see their friends quite often. When they were in their own room they found that Ricky Allen and her roommate joined them frequently. The girls were fast becoming friends.

Ulrich Allen, Ricky to her friends, was a breezy, friendly girl from the West and there was not a soul in the class who did not know all about her. Her roommate was a quiet, sweet young girl from Georgia. Ricky took pains to see to it that everyone should know about her, too.

Janet declared that Ricky was as clear and as unassuming as the country from which she came. Nevertheless, Janet and Ricky could be seen with heads close together very often, planning mischief or laughing over their latest bit of gossip.

Gale, since the afternoon she had rescued the Dean from the lake, had seen the older woman only once. On that occasion the Dean walked across the campus to the library with her. It was something she would take care not to let happen again, she told herself. It seemed that girls from the sorority house had seen her. The upper classmen looked with the utmost distaste upon such familiarity. They saw to it that Gale should regret such friendliness with the head of the institution. She was teased unmercifully and chided and scoffed at upon every occasion. Most of the girls did it in fun, the fun that upper classmen usually have with a Freshman, but one girl in particular seemed to personally resent Gale.

Marcia Marlette had been one of the very last Juniors to arrive for the semester. She lived in Penthouse Row, the fourth floor, in a room directly over Gale and Phyllis. She had heard the story of Gale and the Dean. She had seen for herself that the Dean did smile and stop to talk with Gale when such occasions presented themselves. She was one of the girls who was voluble in her protestations against the new Dean. She had been favored and especially privileged the two terms before. Now that there was a new Dean and a new regime her privileges were swept away. She was to be no more favored than any other girl. That didn't please Marcia, and since she couldn't very well spite the Dean she decided to torture Gale—supposedly a close friend of Dean Travis.

Gale bore the girls' teasing silently, in amused indifference. She didn't mind the stunts she and Phyllis had to perform to appease their sorority sisters, but from the minute Marcia Marlette appeared on the campus things were different. Gale could bear the other girls' teasing, their songs, their sly pointed remarks, but she couldn't and wouldn't stand for it from Marcia.

"I tell you, Phyl," Gale said stormily, flinging her books onto her desk, "I won't stand for it. I'll—I'll tell Dean Travis."

Phyllis smiled patiently. "Can't do that, Gale. We've got to take it. Our turn will come."

"I know," Gale said. She flung herself upon the bed and glared at the ceiling. "But I will blow up and explode if Marcia Marlette doesn't stay away from me."

"What has she been doing now?"

"Met me after Chemistry class and walked to the house with me—making nasty remarks about the Dean all the while. I'll—I'll slap her face some day," Gale threatened.

"Whoa, there," Ricky Allen murmured, sticking her head in at the open door. "Who is gonna slap who?"

"Are we missing anything?" added Gloria Manson.

Gale sat up and laughed. "I am boiling over with suppressed wrath."

"Only it isn't suppressed any more," Phyllis murmured. "Girls, you see before you a volcano about to erupt."

"Go ahead and erupt," Ricky invited, settling herself comfortably on Phyllis' bed.

"What happened?" Gloria asked sympathetically.

Gale sat on the window sill and took a deep breath of the autumn air. "That awful Junior has been pestering me again. I suppose it is only a matter of months before I become immune to it."

"That awful Junior heard what you said," a voice declared nastily.

Gale put her head out the window and looked up. Marcia Marlette was leaning out her window and grinning with exasperating superiority.

"Perhaps you would like to say it directly to me," she invited.

Gale was not lacking in courage and her anger now made her more daring.

"Certainly I'll say it," she answered firmly. "I said you were pestering me again. So what?"

The Junior's face was more irritating.

"Freshmen are supposed to be polite to upper classmen—especially sorority sisters. Rebellion will cost you a month's special privileges."

"But that isn't fair!" Gale cried indignantly. "I didn't do anything—wait, Marcia——"

But the Junior had disappeared into her room. Gale swung about and confronted the others. She strode to the door, but Phyllis preceded her. With her back against the door Phyllis asked:

"Where are you going?"

"Up to Marcia's room," Gale said hotly. "I'm going to tell her a few things! Things I've been aching to say ever since I first saw her. I'm going——"

"You are going to stay right here," Phyllis said calmly. "Sit down, Gale, and get hold of your temper again. I never saw you so fiery. I don't know what Marcia might have done or said, but I'll wager it was only to make you angry. She wants you to do something like this. You will only injure yourself in the end."

"Ignore Marcia," Ricky advised.

Gale submitted reluctantly to their advice. She knew it was wiser to ignore Marcia's slights and cutting remarks, but just the same she was still angry. Her resentment was growing deeper every hour. Oh, she had taken instant dislikes to people before, but she had never felt so unreasonably, so thoroughly hateful toward another girl. The minute she had seen Marcia stroll into the dining room on the night of the latter's arrival Gale could have told Phyllis she wouldn't like her. Before Marcia ever said a word to her, Gale felt resentment burning within her. She didn't know why. Then, when Marcia started to annoy her and Phyllis, Gale more than ever disliked the Junior. So far she had been successful in hiding it. She avoided all possible contact with Marcia, but after all they were bound to meet sometimes. They sat at the same table at dinner, and it was there Marcia was worst of all. Gale and Phyllis accepted everything she said with a slight smile and silence. That only seemed to make matters more difficult. Marcia was deliberately picking an open quarrel and the upper classmen fully realized the position of the Freshmen. Their attitude softened somewhat and for that the girls were grateful. But it still did not solve the question of Marcia.

"Are you going out for hockey?" Gloria asked, idly thumbing Gale's Chemistry book.

"Sure," Ricky declared, "aren't we, Phyl?"

"I am," Phyllis said. "How about you, Gale?"

"For class hockey? The first meeting is tomorrow afternoon." With difficulty Gale turned her attention to other things.

"We only have five minutes before dinner," Gloria announced next.

Ricky dragged herself upright. "Shall we go downstairs and wait?"

Phyllis flung a hasty glance at Gale. If they went downstairs now Marcia would most likely be there. It would be bad enough at dinner with her sitting across from them.

"No," Phyllis said vaguely, "I want to brush my hair and——"

"You had better hurry," Gale murmured.

Phyllis remained close to Gale when they descended the stairs behind Ricky and Gloria. The girls were moving toward the dining room. Phyllis looked hastily around for Marcia. She was not in sight. When Phyllis slipped into her seat beside Gale she looked across the table. Marcia's chair was empty.

"Where's Marcia?" she murmured to the girl on her other side.

"She has permission to eat at the West Campus Dormitory," was the answer.

Phyllis sighed with relief. She did not want to see a quarrel between Gale and Marcia. It would mean only trouble for Gale. Marcia was used to having her own way, girls naturally catered to her. She would not stand to be ignored by a Freshman. That Gale should be friends with the Dean was all the more reason for Marcia to resent her. Last year Marcia had been close to the old Dean. Marcia had had special privileges. She had not been tied to the college grounds to observe the rules as the other girls had. But now Dean Travis did not grant Marcia those special privileges. Phyllis believed that was all that stood between the Dean and popularity with some girls. A lot of the girls wanted special privileges and the Dean did not grant them. Phyllis could not help but admire the Dean for treating all the girls exactly the same. There would be even more dissatisfaction if some girls were allowed to do things and others weren't.

Phyllis, upon learning that Gale and Marcia would not possibly meet tonight and quarrel, was gay with relief.

"I know how you feel," Gale murmured to her friend. "But you really shouldn't have worried, Phyl. I would never make a scene here—before all the others."

"Are you a mind reader? How did you know what I was thinking?" Phyllis demanded.

Gale laughed. "You are an open book to me," she giggled.

Phyllis sighed. "Woe is me! Nothing is a secret any more."

The girls did not linger with the others long after dinner. They went to their room, Phyllis to read and Gale to write letters. She owed one to her parents, one to Miss Relso, who was still taking an interest in their school life, and one to Brent Stockton. The one to Brent was the longest and well it should be. Gale did not often see the young aviator with whom she was so much in love, but their letters were long and frequent and filled with many pictures.

"Send Brent my love," Phyllis told her as she struggled into her pajamas. "Doesn't that make you jealous?" she wanted to know teasingly.

"No," Gale said promptly. "I even sent him a picture of you—and me," she added.

"Foiled!" Phyllis murmured, smothering a yawn in the pillow, "Aren't you ever going to bed?"

"Lights-out bell hasn't rung yet," Gale reminded her.

"You can go to bed anyway," Phyllis informed her. "The Dean won't mind."

"Go to sleep," Gale laughed.

The moonlight came into the room with illuminating brilliance. The girls slept peacefully, sweetly dreaming delightful dreams. The campus was still with the peace of an autumn night. The sorority house was dark. It was as if another world of glorious peace and accord had opened where previously had been the trill of voices and patter of running feet. Now nothing moved but the silent clouds over the moon and the gentle sifting of leaves in the wind.

But suddenly the night was shattered by a bell, a bell riotous and loud, somewhere close to the ear of the sleeping Phyllis. She sprang out of bed with a shriek. Gale sat up and put her hands over her ears. Another bell joined the first and together their voices made a clatter that disturbed sleepers all over the building. Phyllis dashed wildly about, seeking the cause of the clatter. She found an alarm clock under the bed, whose bell was the cause of the initial outburst. She turned it off while Gale sought the second bell. But Gale had no sooner found the clock hidden in her suitcase than another bell broke forth and another and another. The place was alive with bells, each louder and more shrill than the one before.

The girls sat in the center of the floor and looked helplessly at one another.

"Let 'em ring," Phyllis advised.

"That's all we can do," Gale conceded laughingly. "I wonder whose idea this was?"

"What?"

"I said——" Gale began to repeat patiently, but it was no use. Phyllis could not hear her above the clatter. It seemed a million bells were ringing. Never had the girls heard such a varied assortment of bell sounds.

Gradually the bells began to stop. Gently the tinkling died out and the girls climbed back into bed. But they were no sooner settled than the loudest and most disturbing gong of all started.

"Sounds like a fire alarm," Phyllis shouted.

She was hastily rummaging in her closet. Her search disclosed a big alarm clock hidden in a hat box. She brought it out.

"How do you shut it off?" she yelled to Gale.

Gale shook her head, laughing. The two tried everything, but the most effective was stuffing the clock under two pillows. That softened its siren shriek somewhat.

"What a night!" Phyllis groaned, as she climbed back into bed. She very slowly and carefully stuffed cotton in her ears. "I am going to sleep the rest of the night even if the roof caves in!" she prophesied.

"What was going on in your room last night?" Ricky demanded the next morning when she paid them a visit before breakfast.

"Somebody hid a hundred alarm clocks in here to scare us," Phyllis explained, crawling from under Gale's bed. She had discovered two more clocks.

"Going to start a store?" Gloria asked, motioning to the array of clocks standing on Phyllis' desk.

Phyllis shook her head. She opened the door and pushed a chair out into the hall. On it she set all the clocks. In front of them she put a sign "To be claimed," and then they all went down to breakfast.

"Look!" Ricky pointed dramatically to the chair when they returned to get their books for classes.

The chair was empty. The clocks were all gone.

Chapter IV

TROUBLE AHEAD

Gale tucked her books under her arm and started down the steps of Happiness House.

"Gale! Wait!" Adele Stevens called and fell into step beside her. "Even Seniors go to classes sometimes," she smiled. "Nice morning, isn't it?"

"Very," Gale agreed.

"Last night was a nice night, too," the Senior said, with twinkling eyes.

Gale laughed. "Yes. The sound of a million bells always lends enchantment to an autumn night."

Adele laughed, too. "You and Phyllis have been good sports, Gale. Don't think we haven't noticed it."

"We've gotten fun out of it, too," Gale said.

"You are the kind of girls we want in Happiness House," the Senior declared. "But," she frowned, "Gale, we are sorry for some things——"

"Freshmen expect a lot," Gale said, smiling.

"I mean—such as Marcia Marlette."

"Oh." Gale looked across the campus, letting her eyes dwell on the red and golden brown of the leaves stirring in the breeze.

"Gale, don't ever think that the things she does have the approval of the whole sorority," Adele continued seriously. "She is one of our members, true. She was elected to our house when she was a Freshman. Now we can't exactly put her out—it wouldn't be the nice thing to do and she won't quit of her own accord. She knows we don't like what she has been doing lately. Our sorority house is Happiness House. We want to keep it that. We don't want quarrels or bickering. We want friendship between the girls, friendship that lasts much longer than our college days. Do you see what I mean?"

Gale nodded. "I think so."

"Well, I leave you here. Remember, Gale, you and Phyllis are the sort of girls we want in Happiness House—and we hope you want to stay there."

Gale watched the Senior enter the Hall where she was to attend her class. Slowly Gale strolled along to her own class. She liked Adele Stevens.

"Was our noble president giving you some good advice?" a voice asked dryly.

Gale merely glanced at Marcia Marlette as the girl walked beside her. "Yes."

"Thought so. I suppose you think she is just the noblest person," Marcia laughed. "Freshmen always take to Adele. They plan to be like her, but then Freshmen are idealistic and——"

"I've got to go," Gale said, and hastily ran up and into the nearest building. Inside she stood in the shadows until Marcia had turned away and was almost out of sight. Then she came out and went on more peacefully to her own class.

Gale was finding college life more and more interesting. She did want to make something of her life and she seriously thought of studying medicine. She didn't want to be a nurse—rather a doctor. The other girls were inclined to treat such ambition with lightness. They didn't think much of women doctors, but Gale was still determined. Whether she would achieve her doctor's degree was dim in the future, but at least she had chosen to take the pre-medical course at college. She figured that was a step in the right direction.

Her favorite subject right now was Chemistry. She found Professor Lukens, the Chemistry teacher, willing to answer all and any questions. Often she lingered after classes for a further talk or experiment. On one occasion Doctor Norcot was there and the three of them had a most interesting talk until the Dean and Professor Powell, assistant Chemistry teacher, arrived.

"I came for you," the Dean said to the Doctor. "My secretary was suddenly taken ill. She is in the infirmary and the nurse advised calling you."

"I'll come at once," the Doctor said.

Gale, too, gathered up her books and made her way to the door. There the Dean joined her.

"Gale, I haven't seen you for a week or more."

"No," Gale agreed.

The Freshman went down the stairs with the Dean and the Doctor. They stopped on the steps outside to talk before separating. Gale was talking to the Dean when the Doctor suddenly pushed them roughly to one side.

"Look out!" she shouted.

There was a tinkle of glass and a dark stain spread on the stone steps at their feet. The three bent over it before the Doctor whirled and ran into the building.

"A test tube of acid!" Gale cried in amazement. "I wonder how that came to fall out the window?"

"Fall? Perhaps it was thrown," the Dean murmured, looking up at the windows to the Chemistry room which fronted on the campus.

"Thrown!" Gale gasped. "But if that had hit one of us—the way acid burns we might have been scarred for life! No one would do such a thing!"

"No," the Dean agreed unenthusiastically, "no one would do such a thing."

Gale looked at her strangely. The Dean was white, whether with fear or anger, Gale did not know. From the Dean, Gale looked at the shattered glass and up at the window. Doctor Norcot was leaning out, looking directly down at them. She disappeared and a few minutes later rejoined them on the campus. Her face was sternly set and she answered the Dean's questioning glance with a shake of her head.

"There was no one in the room—and the test tubes and materials are all locked in the closet."

The Dean flashed a glance at Gale, The Doctor smiled in understanding.

"Shall we go on to the infirmary now?" she asked.

A few minutes later Gale was walking across the campus toward the field in back of the tennis courts where the Freshman class was practicing hockey. So deeply in thought was she that she passed several girls from the sorority house without recognizing them at all. That night she talked the whole affair over with Phyllis.

"Do you think the Dean actually suspects that the acid was thrown?" Phyllis asked in consternation. "That is an awful thing for anybody to do!"

Gale frowned. "That is what she said. Remember, too, that somebody cut her canoe adrift and she was almost caught in the rapids."

"It would seem somebody doesn't like the new Dean," Phyllis murmured. "Do you know what was wrong with her secretary?"

Gale shook her head. "No, but I am going to find out. I have a hunch that the three incidents are tied together in some way."

"Ah! Mystery at Briarhurst!" Phyllis said gayly. "But both things might have been accidental, you know."

"I don't think so," Gale said firmly. "A rope doesn't cut itself and secondly, a test tube of acid doesn't walk from a locked closet and fall out the window."

"Then you think someone is really trying to injure the Dean?"

"It looks like it," Gale said. She crossed to the window. Her studies were forgotten, the open text book on her desk did not exist. "Heavenly night, Phyl."

From the campus below floated up a chorus of friendly voices. The Seniors were singing their sorority song:

"Secure in love and laughter,
Our voices blend on high,
We link our hands in friendship,

The girls of Omega Chi."

"So far so good," Phyllis said, putting her arm about Gale and leaning with her on the window sill.

"What? The song?"

"No, I mean us. We've been here three weeks now and like it more every day. At least I do," she added.

"Let's go and see Janet and Carol," proposed Gale mischievously.

"It is study hour," Phyllis returned. "Freshmen are supposed to slave away over their books. We are to remain indoors." She continued with twinkling eyes, "How shall we get out? By the back door?"

Gale switched out the light. On tiptoe the girls went to the rear stairs. With the silence of shadows they descended to the ground. Once outside they stood for several minutes in the shadows of the building, waiting for the Seniors to disappear from view. Finally they were safely away from the sorority house. Quickly they ran to the dormitory building where Janet and Carol were housed. Once there, another problem presented itself.

"How'll we get in?" Phyllis wanted to know.

There were two Juniors sitting on the steps in front of the building so that was closed to them. Gale pointed suggestively to a trellis from which only lately the dried vines had been cut to leave room for new growth in the spring.

"Acrobats, eh?" Phyllis giggled. "Well, why not? We used to climb ropes in gym at High School. I guess we can climb that to the second floor. It is a good thing they don't live on the fourth," she added in a stage whisper as she rested halfway to their goal.

Carol and Janet were bent over their books. Out of the corner of her eye Carol saw a head slowly appearing at the open window.

"Help! Burglars!" she shrieked.

"Shshsh," Phyllis laughed. "It is only us."

"Such hospitality," Gale said disgustedly, climbing into the room after Phyllis. "You should have a stepladder at least for your callers."

"Our callers don't usually enter through the window," Janet returned. "Am I glad to see you! I was about to burst with all the biology I am cramming into my head."

"I don't see how she does it," added Carol lightly. "Bugs, bugs——"

"Speaking of bugs," Janet put in, "when does the Freshman team play the Sophomores in hockey?"

"Next week," Phyllis answered.

Noiselessly the door opened. Valerie and Madge stole into the room.

"Ah, a family reunion," Janet beamed. "We will have to celebrate. Carol, get the chocolate."

"We have a box of cookies in our room," added Madge generously.

"Ah, perhaps we had better go to your room," Carol declared brightly.

"I'll bring them here," Madge offered.

Neither the hot chocolate nor the cookies lasted very long when once the six girls set seriously about the task of devouring them.

"You know," Janet said, munching the icing off her cookie before she ate the rest of it, "I heard that one of the Chemistry teachers is sending the Dean candy and flowers."

"Mmmmm," Carol hummed.

"Romantic idiots!" Madge called them. "Because the Dean is young and good looking you think there is a romance."

"Well, why not? Even college professors aren't immune to it. Look at Gale ——" Janet offered mischievously. "Even she was conquered by a birdman."

"That isn't all about the Dean," Valerie said in a whisper and the others leaned forward in interest. "I heard someone is trying to murder her—or something."

"What do you mean?" Gale asked tensely. "Tell us!"

"I heard," Valerie said, "that her house was set afire yesterday."

"What?" Both Phyllis and Gale were on the edge of their chairs with renewed interest. "How?"

"No one knows," Valerie replied. "The maid saw the curtains blazing in the library. She called the caretaker and he ripped them down and stamped the fire out. There was nothing they could have caught fire from. It must have been done deliberately."

"But who?" Carol scoffed. "Why?"

"Things like that aren't done," Janet added. She looked at Phyllis and Gale. "You two look as though you actually believed it."

"Tell them what you know, Gale," Phyllis advised. "But," she added, "you mustn't go around telling the other girls. We can't prove anything—it is only what we think."

"We'll be as mum as mice," Carol promised. "If we have been missing anything, tell us!"

Gale told them of the things she had discovered and of the things she suspected. The other girls were astounded.

"We will have to appoint ourselves solvers of the mystery," Carol suggested.

"We are the best mystery-solvers at Briarhurst," added Janet. "But where do we begin? There aren't any clues or anyone to suspect."

"Good detectives find those things," Madge informed her.

"But for goodness sake," cautioned Phyllis, "be careful about it. Dean Travis might not like our bothering with her affairs. After all, it isn't our business, you know."

"We'll make it our business," Gale proposed.

"And it might mean adventures for us," added Valerie.

"We have been falling rather low on adventures," commented Janet. "Things have been too quiet. We must stir something up."

"We will do that, never fear," prophesied Carol.

"And now we have to go back to the sorority house," Phyllis said, consulting Janet's desk clock. "Lights-out bell rang twenty minutes ago."

"Perhaps we can use the front door instead of the window this time," suggested Phyllis.

Gale and her friend cautiously descended to the campus and there took a deep breath of relief. They had gotten out of the dormitory house without detection, but now to get back into their own room!

They sped across the campus, keeping in the shadows. Almost at the very door of the sorority house they were forced to halt. Crouching in the shadows of the shrubbery they waited while two figures strolled toward them. Two women stopped directly in front of them. One was speaking and they recognized the voice of the Dean.

"But don't you see—that candy was meant for me. If Miss Horton became ill eating it——"

The doctor nodded. "You had a narrow escape. You don't know who sent it to you?"

They continued on their way and the girls glanced at one another. When they had safely and secretly entered Happiness House by the rear door which they had left unlocked when they went out and were again in their room Phyllis smiled:

"I guess your hunch was correct."

"Mmm," Gale murmured, staring into the darkness as she lay in bed. "Do you suppose they were talking about her secretary? If so, she became ill eating candy that was originally sent to the Dean."

"Poisoned?" Phyllis hazarded.

"I don't know." Gale raised herself on one elbow and looked across at Phyllis. "Do you remember Janet saying one of the Chemistry teachers was sending her candy?"

"Say——" Phyllis sat up suddenly. "Chemistry Professor, acid, poisoned candy—they all fit together."

"We aren't sure the candy was poisoned, but that is what I was thinking," Gale murmured. "However, there are four Chemistry professors."

"The question is which one of them threw the acid and poisoned the candy," Phyllis agreed. She yawned. "I am afraid the puzzle will have to wait until morning. This detective is getting sleepy."

Gale wanted to lie awake and think over the puzzling circumstances surrounding the Dean and her reign at Briarhurst, but she didn't, and it was to be many weeks before the mysterious occurrences were solved.

Chapter V

THE HOCKEY GAME

The Freshman class proved to have a very fine hockey team. The girls, including Phyllis, Gale, Ricky and Gloria, were all very agile, swift and determined. The spirit of coöperation which existed between the members of the team was largely responsible for their victories. They made goal after goal in perfectly timed coöperation. They triumphed over the Sophomore team with such a crushing score that the whole Freshman class was delighted and held a party in their honor.

Then came the election of class president. Phyllis, to her astonishment and delight, was elected the Freshman president. Valerie was elected secretary. Altogether, the Adventure Girls were delighted to think two of their number held offices in the class.

The room in Sunshine Alley became the headquarters for all sorts of meetings to discuss class activities. There was scarcely any time at all when someone wasn't there.

Still, with the activities of her office, Phyllis found time to practice with the Freshman hockey team. They practiced often and diligently. The team was next scheduled to play the Junior class and that, they were sure, would be more difficult than the Sophomores. For one thing, Marcia Marlette was on the Junior team. That fact made Gale sure of a difficult encounter.

As the days went by the Adventure Girls could discover nothing new about the strange events that had occurred to the Dean. Gradually their interest began to fade. Occasionally Gale saw the Dean and Doctor Norcot, but even she learned nothing new.

Gale left the Chemistry class on this afternoon without a moment's wasted time and went to the gymnasium and the lockers. There the girls were gathering for the pending hockey game between the two classes. Some of the girls were already in their playing suits and Gale hastened into hers. Phyllis helped her into the pads which, as goalie, Gale needed. Phyllis, in her position of forward, preferred to wear as little protection as possible. She considered herself agile enough to dodge the flying sticks when in a tussle for the ball and was of the opinion that the shin-guards only deterred her when she was in a hurry.

There was a big turnout for the game. Janet and Carol had elected to try out for the cheer leaders' club and they were on duty this afternoon to see that their class should get a large measure of support from the fans.

Gale and the opposing Junior took their positions at the goals. The teams were in line and the game began. The fans cheered lustily on the slightest provocation but there was no goal scored.

Marcia Marlette was playing a brilliant game, even the Freshmen had to admit that. She was here and there and everywhere. She had the ball headed toward the goal every chance she got. Once Gale parried a desperate shot of Marcia's that would have meant the first score had it been a little harder and a little straighter.

But the Junior team did not have the same spirit of coöperation that characterized the younger girls. Marcia was playing for personal glory. The girls could all see that. More than once, if Marcia had passed the ball to a team mate who was in the clear, a score might have been made, but she preferred to play it herself and each time irrevocably lost.

Such was not the case with Phyllis and her team mates, however. They did not hesitate to pass to one another. They were not playing for their own brilliant performances, rather for the game. They wanted their team to win and they did everything in their power to make it so. So unconquerable was their enthusiasm that the score mounted in favor of the Freshmen. Goal after goal was made.

"Lucky for us, Marcia isn't particularly brilliant," Janet told Carol on the sidelines. "If she didn't want to be the whole show herself, the Juniors would easily win over us."

"Treason in the Freshman class!" Carol frowned upon her. "Don't you think we have a good team?"

"Of course," Janet said. "But look at Marcia. She is casting daggers from her greenish eyes at Phyl. One would think there was no one else on the field but Marcia and Phyllis. They have been watching and checkmating each other all afternoon."

"She would dearly love to wrap her stick around Phyllis' neck—or Gale's," giggled Carol. "There they go!"

Marcia and a class mate were dribbling the ball ever closer to the Freshman goal. Gale was on guard. Phyllis and Ricky swept in to rescue the ball and save the game.

There was a sudden mix-up of flying sticks, arms and legs. Two of the players sprawled into the goalie. Gale had a fleeting vision of Marcia Marlette striking out viciously with her stick before she went down under the impact of another Junior.

Gale scrambled to her feet. The others did likewise—that is all but Phyllis. She lay perfectly still, her one leg twisted under her. Janet and Carol dashed out from the sidelines. A sudden hush had fallen over the spectators.

"Phyl!" Gale cried and dropped beside her friend.

"What's the matter?" Doctor Norcot and Professor Lukens had appeared from among the spectators.

After a brief examination by the doctor, Professor Lukens picked Phyllis up in his arms and started toward the infirmary with her.

Gale tore off the padding of her position and ran after them.

"But the game——" mildly protested a Junior.

"Get another goalie," directed Gale and was gone.

Gale was forced to wait in the doctor's office. She wriggled impatiently in the uncomfortable leather chair. Getting to her feet she walked restlessly to the window and around the room. There were a lot of medical books here which at another time would have interested her immensely. However, now she could think of nothing but Phyllis, of the whiteness of her friend's face and the stillness with which she had lain on the field.

The door knob turned and the doctor came into the room. She was in the white clothes of her profession and wore the professional smile.

"Phyl——" Gale said.

"She'll be all right," the doctor assured her, "but her leg is fractured."

"B-Broken?" Gale managed to whisper.

Doctor Norcot nodded. "She must have been hit with a hockey stick—a vicious hit."

"But she will be all right?" Gale insisted.

"After a few weeks she will be as good as new," the doctor promised. "Would you like to see her?"

"Oh, yes!"

Gale found Phyllis awake and grumbling. The sight of her friend made Gale's heart twinge with pity. Phyllis was trying so hard to be brave.

"I've climbed ivy trellises, even jumped out of an airplane with a parachute—and I break my leg playing in a hockey game," Phyllis said disgustedly. "A fine class president you picked!"

"We picked a good one!" Gale said quickly. "We——"

"In here?" a voice said and the door was opened.

"Hi," Janet said.

"We came as quickly as we could when we thought we could see you," added

Carol.

"Who won the game?" Phyllis demanded.

"We did," Ricky said, "because you played so well before——"

"Before Marcia Marlette cracked you with her hockey stick," Janet added savagely.

"She didn't do it," Phyllis said wearily. "No one can say who did it. Sticks were flying in all directions."

Janet said nothing more but she and Gale exchanged significant glances. The girls did not stay long after that. It was evident that Phyllis was tired and they thoughtfully took their leave early, but Phyllis detained Gale long after the others. Gale held her friend's hand until Phyllis was asleep then she softly left the room.

Slowly, deep in thought, Gale stepped from the infirmary building to the campus. A chill night wind had sprung up. She turned toward the gymnasium. She was still in her hockey suit. She would have to go to the lockers and change before going to the sorority house.

Dinner had been an hour ago but she scarcely missed the comfort of her meal. She had been so worried about Phyllis she did not realize how time had flown past. Finding the janitor was an easy task. He unlocked the door to the gymnasium for her and she wasted no time in going to the lockers for her things. Stepping again onto the campus, now warm in her woollen jacket, Gale caught sight of the Dean crossing the campus to her home. Dean Travis beckoned to Gale and waited until the Freshman joined her.

"How is your friend?" she asked immediately.

Gale told her.

"You missed your dinner, didn't you?" the Dean continued. "Come home with me. We will dine together."

"Oh, but I——" Gale began confusedly.

"Forget I am the Dean for this one night," Dean Travis invited humorously. She smiled and Gale could not resist. "I've wanted to talk with you often, Gale. You aren't merely one of the Freshmen to me, you know. You are a friend."

Gale found the living room of the Dean's home cozy and warm. A wood fire burned in the fireplace. She sat on the divan before it and let the warmth of the flames ease away some of the nervousness she still felt from her worry over Phyllis. The dinner was the best she had had at Briarhurst, at least she enjoyed it the most. She talked to the Dean as she might have to one of the girls. There was no stiffness or formality between them. She found herself telling the Dean about Phyllis and about the letter she, Gale, must write when she returned to the sorority house. It was a letter to Phyllis' aunt, the cold, austere woman who was paying Phyllis' tuition at Briarhurst. Gale did not like Miss Fields. She resented the way the woman so completely dominated Phyllis' life and the blind obedience she exacted from the girl.

It was late when Gale got back to the sorority house. Adele Stevens met her at the door.

"How is Phyllis?"

Gale told her all the details she could and together they walked up to Gale's room. There the sorority president stopped to chat a while. When she left Gale found it lonesome. It would be hard to get used to living alone for a few weeks. Phyllis was always so gay, so friendly and understanding, Gale would certainly miss her.

She sat down at her desk to write to Miss Fields. It was the most difficult task she had ever had to do. She didn't like Phyllis' aunt and her letter was not the friendly, sympathetic epistle it might have been had she been writing to one of the other girls' mothers. When she finished she read the note through. It was decidedly stiff and unfriendly. She tore it up and began another. She finally enclosed her fifth attempt in an envelope and stamped it. She was sure Phyllis would receive scant sympathy from Miss Fields. The woman, in all the years since Phyllis was small, had given the girl no obvious affection, no love. Phyllis always had been afraid of her, always had to obey her blindly and implicitly. Gale remembered how difficult it had been for Phyllis to come to Briarhurst with the rest of the Adventure Girls. And now this had to happen! How would Miss Fields accept the news? That worried Gale quite as much as it did Phyllis.

Standing at the window, watching shadows moving slowly on the campus as clouds drifted past the moon, Gale thought of what Janet had said that afternoon. Had Marcia deliberately hit Phyllis with her hockey stick? Gale's more charitable nature rebelled at the thought. Marcia might be selfish, stubborn, not at all likeable, but surely she wouldn't do anything like that!

The Freshmen had won the game but at what a cost. Her zeal for the game would cost Phyllis days of suffering and weeks of inactivity that would be even harder to bear. Mentally Gale made a promise to help Phyllis all she could.

Chapter VI

A NOTE

"Surprise!" Phyllis said gaily.

Gale stared in amazement. Phyllis was in her own bed in their room in Sunshine Alley yet she hadn't been there that morning. Doctor Norcot stood beside the bed smiling. Adele Stevens was on the other side.

"Phyl!" Gale stuttered. "What—why—how—my dear, I'm so glad to see you!"

"She wouldn't give me a moment's peace until I said she could come back here," Doctor Norcot explained, smiling.

"I'll get well twice as quickly here," Phyllis declared. "I feel a hundred per cent better already."

"Sunshine Alley will cure her," Adele Stevens laughed.

When the doctor and Adele were gone Gale sat beside Phyllis and hugged her.

"Gee, I'm glad to have you back. If you hadn't come soon I would be talking to myself."

"Tell me everything that has happened in these weeks," Phyllis demanded. "Who has done what and why?"

"Well, the teacher gave us a corking examination in Biology today but I don't know why," Gale laughed.

"I suppose it was to see how brilliant you were," Phyllis smiled. "Gale! Guess what! Monday I start classes again. I'll have to go on crutches for a while but at least I won't have to stay in one room any longer. Isn't it marvelous?"

"We'll have a party and celebrate," Gale proposed. "I'll tell Janet and Carol to come over. Let them climb our trellis this time. I'll make fudge and——"

"Wait a minute! You take my breath away," Phyllis declared. "Oh, Gale, you have no idea how lonesome it was over there in the infirmary."

"I know how lonesome it was here," Gale countered. "This was bad enough. All by myself at night, I'd dream I saw ghosts—I almost moved over to the infirmary to be with you," she laughed.

"I hear that the Dean has started the work on the stables for the horses we are to have in the spring," Phyllis said. "We will have a lot of fun riding. Remember that summer in Arizona?"

"We'll have fun if we can stay on the horses," Gale giggled. "Ricky is an authority on the subject and she doesn't know we can ride so she has been giving us some lessons."

"Without horses?"

"We use chairs and things," Gale explained, "but a real live horse will be more difficult to handle than a chair with a pillow on it."

"Rightly spoken, my friend," Ricky herself declared, entering unannounced at that moment. "Phyllis! You're back! Gee! Hi, Glory," she shouted across the hall to her roommate, "look who is here! Our star hockey player is back!"

Sunshine Alley became alive with figures eager to welcome Phyllis back. The Freshman president had been sadly missed.

That night the room was the scene of a secret rendezvous of the Adventure Girls. Valerie and Madge had managed to unobtrusively sneak out of their dormitory house with Janet and Carol. A light hidden under a tilted wastepaper basket enabled just enough light to escape to dispel the darkness while the girls sat around and talked in whispers and ate Gale's fudge.

"Has anybody heard anything more about strange things happening to the Dean?" Phyllis asked.

The others shook silent heads. However, Janet spoke up.

"I was in French class late the other day and when I came out two teachers were talking in the hall. I dropped my book accidentally and while I was picking it up I couldn't help but hear what they said. It was strange."

"Well? What did they say?" Carol inquired lazily.

"One said 'Then the President hasn't yet discovered who took the money from the fund?'"

"Yes?" Gale and Phyllis leaned forward.

"The other one said 'No.' Then they saw me and walked away."

"You scared them," Carol accused.

"What do you suppose they meant?" Madge murmured.

"By a simple act of deductive reasoning I have come to the conclusion that there is a crook loose on the campus," Janet announced.

"Did you think of that all by yourself?" Carol chided.

"Someone took money from the school funds?" Gale murmured. "Things are getting worse."

"Why don't they call a policeman?" Carol asked, juggling a book on her head.

"And get the college name spread over every newspaper in the country? That would be a nice scandal for the school!" Janet scoffed.

"It's better than having our things disappear from under our very noses," Carol retorted.

"No one has touched any of the students' things," Valerie reminded them. "It seems to be the college and the Dean who are in difficulty."

"I wonder who is doing it?" Phyllis murmured. "It must be someone in the college."

"Did you see Marcia Marlette this afternoon?" Carol started to giggle. "Where was she going? She was dressed in all her finery."

"She had everything on but the kitchen sink," added Janet with a laugh.

"I hear that Professor Lukens, the Chemistry teacher, has conferences with her after classes sometimes," Madge murmured.

"He has with Gale, too," Valerie smiled.

"Aha! Rivals!" Carol jeered and dodged a magazine thrown by Gale.

"How about the stables going up over behind the Chemistry Hall? Wait until I dash down College Avenue on a pure white steed——" Carol began theatrically.

"You will fall off," Janet said dryly.

Carol made a face at her. "How do you get down from a horse?" she inquired sagely.

"Jump," offered Janet.

"Step down," Madge said.

"You don't, you get it from a duck," Carol said sweetly.

Janet choked on her fudge. Madge threw a handy pillow while Carol took refuge behind Phyllis.

"In case you don't know," she continued, "down is what you stuff pillows with."

"You don't have to explain," Janet said distastefully. "After that terrible pun I think I had better take you back to the dormitory. Come along, infant."

"See you tomorrow, Phyl," Valerie said in parting.

"But I don't want to go to bed yet," protested Carol.

"Shshsh," Gale warned. She listened at the door. "Someone is coming."

"Where'll we hide?" whispered Janet frantically.

Carol dived under the bed. Janet did likewise while Valerie and Madge ran to the closet. Gale put the light out and hopped into her bed. Innocent silence settled down over the room. Footsteps halted at the door. Cautiously the doorknob turned, but the door did not open. Instead, something white was shoved under the door. When the footsteps had retreated along the corridor again the girls cautiously came out of hiding.

"Now go ahead and sneeze!" Janet stormed at Carol. "If we had been discovered it would have been your fault. You always have to sneeze at the strangest times!"

"I can't help it," Carol giggled. "You tickled me."

"We had better get out before we are discovered," Madge whispered fearfully.

"Wait until we see what is in the note," Janet proposed. "Open it, Gale."

Gale lit the light again, under its protective shield, and picked up the square white envelope lying on the floor. She turned it over in her hand. There was no address upon it. She tore it open and while the other girls waited read the few words. She stared retrospectively at the floor.

"Well?" Carol hissed. "Is it a secret?"

"What? Oh——" Gale turned to the note again. "It says 'Do not interfere in affairs that are none of your concern.'"

"Is that all?" Carol said in disappointment. "No—no threats?"

"What can it mean?" Phyllis whispered to Gale.

"Just what it says," Janet declared bluntly. "We are to mind our own business —or else."

"Or else what?" Carol demanded.

"Mind our own business," Madge repeated. "But what have we interfered in?"

"True," Valerie admitted. "We haven't done anything."

Gale sat on the bed beside Phyllis. "I wonder if this was meant only for you and me—or for all of us," she murmured.

"No one knows we are here tonight—at least I hope no one knows," Janet said.

"It is obvious someone doesn't want us to discover something," Phyllis murmured.

"But what?" Carol insisted. "Mixed up, I call it."

"You're always mixed up," Janet said loftily. "Can't you understand, darling, that whoever wrote this note is afraid of us?"

"We aren't that bad looking," Carol protested humorously. "What are they afraid of?"

"I wish we knew," Gale said. "However, now that we are accused of prying into whatever it is, we will really do some prying."

"I'll sleep with my eyes and ears wide open," Carol promised.

The girls took their leave then, sneaking as noiselessly as possible down the corridor and out the back door of the building. Gale went downstairs with them, locked the door and returned to her room. She found Phyllis still awake and pondering the strange note.

"Who left it, Gale?" she asked.

Gale shook her head. "I wish I knew. It might make things clearer."

"At any rate, we must know something that we shouldn't," Phyllis said wisely. "What will we do about it?"

Gale ran restless fingers through her curls. "I don't know, Phyl. I was beginning to think things were calming down. Now this——"

"Stirs them up again," Phyllis said. "You had better go to bed, Gale, you are tired."

"And you, Phyl," Gale said contritely. "This has been a day for you, hasn't it? The Doctor would scold if she knew you have had scarcely any rest since this morning."

"Bother the Doctor," Phyllis said fretfully. "Gale, promise me you won't do anything about that note until I can go with you."

Gale nodded slowly. "When I do something I'll tell you—but I don't know what we could do," she added helplessly.

Chapter VII

NO CLUES

Gale hastily deposited her own and Phyllis' books in their room and went flying downstairs again. Phyllis, out on her new crutches, was waiting for her on the campus. Together the two slowly made their way to the home of the Dean. They had seen her leave the office only a few minutes earlier and hoped she would interview them. Or rather, Gale corrected her thoughts, let them interview her.

The girls had talked things over long and earnestly. They had let several days elapse, but now they had decided the best thing to do was to go to the Dean with the note that had mysteriously appeared in their room.

Gale proposed to tell the Dean everything that the girls knew or suspected—things which the Dean, herself, already knew. The attempts on the Dean had been interpreted by the girls to mean direct attempts to seriously injure her. Now they wanted to know why. Since someone had chosen to link them to the mysterious events, by means of that note, they felt they had a right to share the mystery whatever it was.

Gale was trying to fit the pieces of the puzzle together as they walked along. First there had been the canoe, then the acid hurled from the Chemistry room window, the candy eaten by Dean Travis' secretary—and other things that had come to her ears such as the fire in the Dean's home and the stolen funds from the college treasury. But what was it the girls knew that someone feared? Try as she would, Gale could not think of a thing that pointed directly to any one person. There was no reason anyone should suspect the Adventure Girls of being interested in the Dean's difficulties.

"It is glorious being able to be about again," Phyllis sighed as she rested a moment. "I can hardly wait for the time I'll be able to play hockey again."

"I shouldn't think you would want to play," Gale said laughingly. "You've been so brave, Phyl," she added more seriously.

"Tush!" Phyllis smiled.

But Gale was not deceived. She knew Phyllis well, she knew her friend's moods and lately she had recognized the strain Phyllis was under. The confinement Phyllis had undergone was desperately trying. Phyllis was active, she was full of life. She had to be doing things, accomplishing things to be content. If anything should happen to take away Phyllis' activities and zest for enjoyment, life would not mean much to the girl. The courage she had displayed these past weeks had been strongly aided by the knowledge that with patience she would be able to go back to her old activities again. It was only because she knew her indisposition was but temporary that Phyllis had been able to bear it so cheerfully.

Gale ran lightly up the steps of the Dean's home while Phyllis waited. Steps were difficult for her to negotiate and she would not do it unless she were certain the Dean would see them.

The maid answered Gale's ring. She said the Dean was home and would see them. When the girls were in the living room the Dean entered. She smiled naturally upon Gale and shook hands with Phyllis.

"I'm delighted to see you about again, Miss Elton."

"I'm delighted to be about again," Phyllis said happily.

"Dean Travis, we came to see you because—that is we think——" Gale paused for breath then continued more resolutely, "The day I towed your canoe to shore you made me promise not to mention the subject. I haven't—generally. Since then I've heard of things that have happened to you. What you said made me think the acid was thrown out the window that day and——"

The Dean held up her hand for silence. She was staring past Gale. The Freshman turned. The door behind her was slowly closing.

"Suppose we walk on the campus," the Dean proposed in a low voice. "We can be sure there will be no prying ears there."

"Do you want to wait for us, Phyl?" Gale asked.

"No, indeed!" Phyllis said vigorously. "It may be hard for me to get around but I won't remain behind. I'm not going to miss anything."

The three walked slowly in the direction of the Chemistry Hall in back of which work was being carried on building the new stables. The workmen were finished for the day so the girls and the Dean could inspect the scene while they talked. Lumber was piled high in readiness for the building, the foundation was already dug and the ground was littered with implements and discarded stones and bricks.

The three halted near a pile of lumber. No one was in sight, so Gale continued with the tale she had. When she had finished the Dean looked at both Gale and Phyllis thoughtfully for a moment before she spoke.

"What you say is true," she agreed. "Strange things have been happening, but

I see no reason why you should be connected with me."

"You see," Phyllis put in, "we have always been mystery fans and we have been keeping our eyes and ears open. Perhaps someone found out we were snooping——"

"But we haven't discovered anything," Gale said. "Dean Travis, what about the money that was stolen? Did someone take money from the college funds?"

The Dean nodded slowly. "Since you know so much I will tell you what little more there is to be told. Someone, we don't know who, took money—cash—from the safe in my office. The balance of the money, however, is in the bank and quite safe."

"Haven't you any idea who might have taken it?" Phyllis pursued.

"Four people have the combination, and I am convinced that each one is trustworthy. About the other occurrences—you already know as much as I."

"Why did Professor Harris give up her position as Dean?" Gale asked suddenly. She had for a long time been thinking that the former Dean might be trying to revenge herself upon the new head for taking her position.

"She went abroad to live in England, I believe," Dean Travis said. "She had been planning it for quite a while."

"And then you were appointed," Gale murmured.

"Wasn't there an election or something?" Phyllis asked. "Wasn't there anyone else trying for the position the same time as you?"

"I believe there was," the Dean smiled. "Are you trying to make me believe that my rival for the position has sworn revenge? No, girls, I don't think that is possible."

"What does Doctor Norcot think about these things?" Gale asked.

"She is at quite a loss to explain them," the Dean murmured.

"The day she ran back to the Chemistry room—she saw no one?" Gale continued hopefully. "I'm sorry, Dean, this sounds like a cross examination, doesn't it? We are being terribly nosey, but it is only because we are so interested."

"Since someone is sending us notes it makes us all the more curious," added Phyllis. "I would like to know who sent us that note."

"Do you have it with you?" the Dean asked.

Gale pulled it from her coat pocket and unfolded it.

"You see," she said, "it is typewritten so there is no danger of recognizing the handwriting."

"About every other person at Briarhurst has a portable typewriter," Phyllis frowned. "We are absolutely stumped for clues."

"Aren't you afraid to stay here with so many things happening?" Gale asked the Dean.

The Dean shook her head smilingly. "I've been entrusted with this position and I am going to see it through to the best of my ability. I am going to make Briarhurst an even finer and larger college than it already is. That is, of course, with the coöperation of the girls."

"You have our coöperation," Phyllis said promptly. "All the Adventure Girls and some others are keenly interested in everything you propose—the new organ for the chapel, the new and different classes, the horses for spring riding, all of them. It will be really wonderful. I've always wanted to ride well," she continued softly.

The Dean tapped Phyllis' crutch. "Doctor Norcot tells me it will be only a week or so and you won't have to use these any more. I'm glad."

"So am I," Phyllis said vigorously. "I——"

Her words froze in a cry of horror on her lips. The pile of lumber against which Gale and the Dean were leaning was tottering. Phyllis threw herself forward, shoving and dragging Gale and the Dean clear, but in so doing was herself caught in the avalanche of lumber as it toppled down upon them.

Chapter VIII

MYSTERIOUS STRANGER

Gale could never quite clearly remember her dash to the infirmary after Doctor Norcot, but finally Phyllis was there, shut into a room with the doctor and nurse and Gale and the Dean were in the corridor. Gale was pacing up and down, the Dean watching her. It was dark outside and a single light made a white circle on the tile floor and walls.

Gale stopped her pacing long enough to glare at the door to Phyllis' room. She had a wild desire to throw it open and burst in.

"Be patient a little longer, Gale," the Dean said compassionately. "You can see her in a few minutes."

"Why did it have to be her?" Gale asked in an agonized whisper. "She suffered so much these past weeks after the hockey accident and now—— She did it saving us! We might have been crushed under that lumber."

The door opened and the Doctor came out followed by a nurse.

"May I go in?" Gale asked.

The Doctor nodded wearily. "Be cheerful, make her smile but don't let her get excited or talk too much."

"I'm so full of splinters I can't even smile," Phyllis said gloomily when Gale was beside her. "You had better go get your dinner."

"You aren't going to get rid of me so easily," Gale laughed.

Phyllis' face was all scratched and she looked white and tired.

"Honestly, Phyl——" she began when she remembered the Doctor's warning. "This was a fine thing for you to do. Now I'll be by myself in our room tonight again. See that you are back tomorrow, young lady, or I shall move in here with you. After all, I believe you did it so you wouldn't have to go to Biology class tomorrow. There is more than one way of escaping an exam. Though I can't say I would choose this way."

"Don't talk so much," Phyllis said bluntly. "You don't know a word you are saying."

Gale nodded soberly. "Right you are. I can't think of a thing but the way you pulled us out of danger this afternoon and now you——" She took her friend's hand. "I'll make it up to you sometime, Phyl."

"Go way," Phyllis said tenderly. "Go get your dinner and study your old Biology and come and see me tomorrow."

Gale went out and found the Doctor and the Dean in conference in the corridor.

"She seems to be all right," Gale said.

"She has the courage of six girls," the Doctor said firmly. "But, Miss Howard, I am afraid your friend is right where she was five weeks ago."

"You mean her leg——"

"Crushed under the lumber this afternoon," the Doctor said. "Not too badly crushed but enough to undo the healing of these past weeks."

"Poor Phyllis!" Gale whispered.

"Do you think she would want to go home until she is well again?" the Dean asked as she walked to the door with Gale.

Gale shook her head. "No," she said decidedly. "Phyllis wouldn't want to go home." Strange, perhaps, that she should choose to stay here, but even the college infirmary was brighter, more cheerful than the house on the hill to which Phyllis would have to go.

"Come and have your dinner with me," the Dean invited.

"Thanks, no," Gale said when they were on the campus. "I—I'd rather be alone, thank you. I have to write Phyllis' aunt again," she sighed.

The Dean turned toward her office and Gale toward Happiness House. She walked along, hands in her pockets, deep in thought until at last she reached the sorority house. She met Adele Stevens and Ricky and conveyed to them the news of Phyllis. After her dinner she went upstairs to study but she found she could not concentrate.

Phyllis was on her mind. Alternated with thoughts of her friend were remembrances of the conversation they had had with the Dean that afternoon. She was completely at sea as to who could be doing the mysterious things. Quite suddenly she sat erect before her desk and stared with narrowed eyes at the wall opposite. That had been a goodly pile of lumber this afternoon. It had been piled, perhaps a bit precariously, but nevertheless it had not wavered until that moment before it fell. Could it be—was it possible—that someone had pushed it? The pile really had needed but a bit of pressure to send it over. Who had exerted that bit of pressure?

At first Gale laughed at herself. It was a wild idea! No one would do that! But the more she thought about it the more plausible it became. She had thought no one would throw acid out the Chemistry Hall window—but evidently someone had!

Then she remembered the note the Dean had had in her hand when the lumber fell upon Phyllis. She had a fleeting vision of the same note lying in the mud unheeded. Their one valuable clue gone!

Catching up her coat Gale switched out the light and stepped into the hall. No one was in sight. She sped down the stairs and at the bottom bumped into Adele Stevens.

"Where are you going, Gale?" the Senior asked. "It is study hour."

"I know," Gale said breathlessly. "I—I can't study. I thought I'd go for a short walk."

"Thinking about Phyllis?" Adele said kindly. "All right, Gale. I suppose you can tonight. Be back before lights-out bell."

"I will," Gale breathed and was gone before the sorority president could change her mind.

The late autumn evening was clear and cold. The leafless branches of the trees rubbed together making queer eerie noises. Windows of the dormitory and sorority houses shone yellow with light. Gale stepped along briskly. She passed the dormitory houses and halted before the Chemistry Hall. There was a light burning in the third floor laboratory. Was one of the Professors working late? Probably. She turned away into the shadows behind the building.

It was terribly dark in here. She took the small flashlight from her coat pocket and switched it on. She had been just about to stumble into a mud puddle. Now she jumped across it and proceeded with caution. She came to the scene of the afternoon. The lumber lay as it had fallen. In her mind's eye Gale could still see Phyllis lying there. She shivered and turned away. Carefully she went over the ground. Caught under a board, torn almost in half, Gale found the note. It was dirty and wrinkled and torn but she carefully folded it in the original creases and stored it in her coat pocket. She switched off her flashlight and stood listening. Had she heard a sound?

The moon was completely hidden behind a cloud. The wind whistled in her ears. She shivered in her warm coat. It wasn't the cold, it was the darkness, the shadowy world about her, and the knowledge of another's presence. She strained her ears to catch the faintest sound. There was a sudden creak and a smothered exclamation as someone stumbled over a bit of lumber. Gale crouched against half-piled boards and waited.

A man's figure was outlined against the light from the moving clouds. A hat pulled low on his forehead and a long overcoat with collar turned up completely hid his identity. Gale considered jumping in front of him and flashing her light in his face. She would know who he was then! But she reconsidered the next moment, and waited to see what he was after. It was obvious that he was searching for something. He crouched low to the ground, examining every foot of space thoroughly with a small pocket lamp. What could he be searching for? Could it be the note in her pocket? Convulsively her hand closed about the muddy piece of paper. It must be this! There was nothing else here. Gale took a step backward as the figure moved closer. That was the fatal moment. She stumbled wildly over something and fell. The clatter was distinct and as loud as a cannon shot in the stillness. The man whirled. He flashed his light full into Gale's face. She blinked in the sudden glare and did not move. In another second the light was gone and the figure had fled toward the campus.

Gale scrambled to her feet but it was hopeless to think of pursuit. If only she hadn't fallen! Her clumsiness had spoiled everything! The man was gone now and so was her chance of solving the mystery. She shook the mud from her coat and picked her way back to the campus.

The light was gone from the Chemistry laboratory. A lot of windows in the other dormitories were dark, too. It was growing late. Gale hastened her steps. She had to be in before lights-out bell rang. She had promised Adele, and not only that, she didn't fancy being out late on the campus with that mysterious stranger—the mystery man who knew her identity but whom she did not know. He had her at a decided disadvantage. He knew, now, who was spying on him and noting his movements. She knew she must guard against someone, but whom? If only she had discovered his identity! She rebuked herself again. She would have given nearly all she possessed to know who else wanted the note.

When she returned to her room she examined the bit of paper more closely. Through the dirt, after she had carefully pasted the torn parts together, the brief typewritten message was still clearly legible. There was nothing to distinguish this typewriting from any other except—the letter R was slightly raised above the level of the other letters. That might help a little in identifying the typewriter. If she found a machine which had that little peculiarity it might lead to the mysterious stranger.

She smiled to herself as she switched off her light and got into bed. She would turn all the girls into Sherlock Holmeses seeking and trying all the typewriters they could find.

Chapter IX

BAD NEWS

Noiselessly Gale closed the door behind her. Swiftly her glance traveled over the room. Girls' things were strewn about in disorder. Gale smiled to herself with mingled pride and humor. At least her own room and Phyllis' didn't look like this and this room belonged to Juniors! Cautiously she bent down and looked under the bed. Yes, it was here. She pulled out the black case and snapped back the lid. With nervous fingers she inserted a sheet of paper in the portable typewriter. She typed a few words and tore the sheet out again. She had just snapped the lid and shoved the case beneath the bed once more when she heard voices.

Marcia was returning! Gale ran for the closet. There was no time to slip out of the room without being seen. She hid in the depths behind the dresses. The door was open a crack. She could hear but she could not see what went on in the room.

"Now where did I leave them?" Marcia's voice demanded fretfully.

Another lazy voice belonging to Marcia's roommate inquired:

"Delivering more notes for Professor Lukens?"

"No. It's my Latin notes—here they are! Let's go, we'll be late."

The two girls were gone as quickly and as suddenly as they had come. Gale lost no time in making her way out of their room. She went downstairs to her room where Valerie was waiting for her.

"Did you get it?" Valerie asked.

Gale sank onto the bed and heaved a sigh of relief. "I did, and I nearly got caught. Marcia and her roommate came back while I was there."

"Did they see you?"

Gale shook her head and unfolded the sheet of paper. "I hid in the closet. Now, where is that note?"

"Here." Valerie produced the note which the girls had received under the door.

Carefully the two checked the letters. The letters produced by Marcia's typewriter were even and clear cut. It was evident that the notes had not been produced by the same machine.

Valerie sat back and looked at Gale. "Well?"

Gale shrugged and folded the papers together. "Exhibit A is a failure. We'll try some more."

"We got it!" Carol burst in followed by Janet.

"Is it catching?" Valerie asked.

"Whose is it?" Gale wanted to know.

"The Chemistry Professor's," Carol said proudly.

"And the assistant's," added Janet. "We covered them both. Are we good detectives or are we?"

The check-up of the typing on the last two notes was the same as it had been with Marcia's. None of them were alike and none of them resembled the typing in the mysterious note. The type of the Chemistry Professor's machine was much larger while that of his assistant was smaller.

"Shucks," Carol said disgustedly. "We had all that work for nothing."

"Perhaps it wasn't written by any machine here at the college," Valerie said.

Gale nodded. "True, it might not have been."

"I think it was," Carol said. "There are no visitors on whom we could blame all these mysterious happenings, and certainly the same person is responsible for the notes!"

"We will have to find some more typewriters."

"Tell you what," Janet said, "I've a bright idea. Let's give a party and hold a scavenger hunt. We will make the items for the girls to bring in mostly typewriters. In that way we will have all the typewriters brought to us and we can try them."

"It would immediately make the one person we want suspicious. He could smash his machine then," Carol said. "You will have to have a brighter idea than that."

"My next bright idea is to go and visit Phyllis," Janet said. "All in favor——"

"Aye!" The vote was unanimous.

The girls descended to the campus. It was while they were passing the East Campus Dormitory where Janet and Carol abided that another Freshman hailed them.

"Hi, Carol, the house mistress wants to see you—and she is angry," the girl added confidentially.

"If it is that little matter of a broken window——" Carol began calmly.

"Broken window?" Gale asked. "In your room?"

Janet giggled. "I threw a book at Carol. She dodged and it went through the window."

Valerie shook her head sadly. "A Freshman trick! I am ashamed of you. To think——"

"She wants to see you too," the Freshman said smiling, "about the broken vase in the hall."

"A Freshman trick!" Janet mimicked.

"It was an accident," Valerie said firmly. "I slipped and fell against it. I couldn't help it if the table wiggled and the vase fell off."

"Did it fall or was it pushed?" Carol winked at Janet.

"I suppose I'll have to go in," Valerie sighed.

That left Gale to go on alone to the infirmary to see Phyllis. That young lady was chafing at the delay in her recovery. It was a week now since the second accident and she wanted to get back to Happiness House and on her feet. She did not like the restrictions placed on her by the Doctor and frankly told her so. Doctor Norcot merely smiled and told her to be good.

Gale told Phyllis all the news of the campus and only when it was nearing dinner time did she leave. When she closed the door to Phyllis' room behind her she noticed the Doctor standing in the hall. She beckoned to Gale and the Freshman followed the physician to her office. There Gale sat in the chair facing the Doctor across her desk.

"Is anything the matter?" Gale asked when she noted the tenseness of the Doctor's expression and the frown on the usually smiling features.

The latter nodded gloomily. "There is—a great deal."

"Has anything happened to the Dean?" Gale asked, the mystery still uppermost in her mind.

"No," the Doctor said getting up and pacing to the window. "No, she is quite safe."

"Then it is Phyllis," Gale said with quiet conviction. "What is it? Tell me!"

Doctor Norcot came across and leaned against the corner of the desk at Gale's side.

"What sort of a woman is Miss Elton's aunt?"

Gale was taken somewhat by surprise. Why should she ask about Phyllis' aunt?

"She——" Gale fumbled for words. "She isn't exactly pleasant," she said at last quite frankly. "Cold—aloof—stern. Why?"

"Has she money?" Doctor Norcot asked next.

Gale was more astounded than ever.

"I—I don't know," she said finally. "She keeps a big house—but not lavishly. She is sending Phyllis to college. I suppose she must have."

"Does she love her niece? I mean, would she do anything for Phyllis?"

Gale sat back in her chair and looked squarely at the Doctor.

"I don't understand, Doctor. Why don't you ask Phyllis these things? Why do you want to know?"

"Because——" Doctor Norcot laid her hand gently on Gale's shoulder. "Because unless your friend has an operation she will never walk again—not as other girls."

"Oh!" Gale shrank at the picture presented to her. Phyllis helpless! Phyllis never to run or dance or play with the girls again.

"But isn't there something we can do? I'll do anything!" she told the Doctor passionately. "Anything!"

"An operation will cost money. Unless she has it——"

"Unless she has it," Gale echoed faintly. "How much would you charge for the operation, Doctor?"

"Oh, I wouldn't perform it," the Doctor said. "I'm not a surgeon. But we would have to get a good one—the best in the East. Otherwise she hasn't a chance."

"Have—have you told her?" Gale asked.

"No—quite frankly, I haven't the heart."

"She is so brave," Gale agreed simply. "It is horrible to think——"

"I had to tell you," the Doctor said. "Between us perhaps we can think of something to do."

Gale passed a dazed hand across her eyes. "I can't think of anything right now."

"It has been a shock. We will talk about it again tomorrow."

Gale rose and went to the door. "Do you think we should tell Phyllis yet?"

Doctor Norcot smiled slowly. "Suppose we wait a little while. There is no use to frighten her. When we tell her we might be able to promise her recovery later."

Gale was in a daze as she walked across the campus. Phyllis, the girl who had always been so active, so gay in the face of tremendous odds, was faced now with a sterner bit of life than had yet confronted her. It would take every bit of courage Phyllis possessed to face the news when the Doctor told her.

Gale had no rosy hopes that Miss Fields would help. Phyllis' aunt was not the sort to be generous and kind especially when it hurt herself. If she did not consent to put up the money for the operation Phyllis would suffer. The injustice of it hurt Gale. She was Phyllis' friend, Phyllis had saved her and the Dean at this expense! She must do something! But what? She didn't have the money— none of the girls had. They were helpless, as helpless as Phyllis herself, to do anything.

Gale, instead of going immediately to the sorority house, went down to the village. The long walk was what she needed. The bracing air invested her with a little optimism. After all, Miss Fields couldn't be as harsh as all that! She wouldn't want Phyllis to suffer if she could help. At the railway station Gale sent a telegram to Marchton asking Miss Fields to come to Briarhurst as soon as possible and signed her own name.

Then she walked slowly back up the hill, scorning the ride offered her by the old bus driver. She wanted to be alone and think and not have to listen to his garrulous chatter.

Dinner was in progress when she arrived at Happiness House. Instead of going into the dining room she went upstairs. Once there she flung herself upon the bed and smothered her sobs in the pillow. Her tears were all for Phyllis; for her own helpless position, helpless to aid the friend who had tried to aid her, Gale, in like circumstances; for the friend who had saved Gale serious injury that day from the falling lumber.

"Aren't you hungry?" Ricky demanded bursting in. "My eagle eyes caught sight of you sneaking in just now and I—say, what's the matter? Gale! You aren't sick!"

Gale sat up, wiping away her tears. "Nope."

"Then why the anguish? Bucking Bronchos! Don't tell me you flunked your Biology!"

"Nothing so simple," Gale said.

"Simple? Biology is anything but simple! I never heard of so many bugs back on the ranch," Ricky mourned. "I sometimes wish I had stayed there." She put her arm about Gale. "Tell Auntie what the trouble is."

Haltingly Gale told Ricky everything the Doctor had said.

"We gotta do something," Ricky said. She sniffed. "You'll have me crying too in a minute. Does Phyllis know?"

Gale shook her head. "We don't want her to—yet."

"Then you had better not tell the other girls," Ricky advised wisely. "One of them is sure to let it slip."

Gale nodded. "It will be between you and me. I've telegraphed her Aunt to come. The Doctor can talk to her before we tell Phyllis."

"Come downstairs and have your dinner," Ricky coaxed.

"I'm not hungry."

"Neither am I—now," Ricky sighed. "But we have to eat something. Remember, we have hard classes tomorrow."

Chapter X

MISS FIELDS' VISIT

"I am going with you!" Ricky said firmly. Gale looked at Doctor Norcot helplessly. When Ricky was determined upon a thing nothing could change her mind.

"Why?" Gale ventured.

"I want to see what this female Simon Legree looks like," Ricky said calmly. "You may need my sunny presence to help persuade her."

"There won't be much use for persuasion I'm afraid," Gale said drearily. "Either she has the money or she hasn't."

Yesterday Gale had received a telegram with the news that Miss Fields would be in Briarhurst this afternoon for merely an hour. As a result Doctor Norcot and Gale were going to the railroad station to meet her when Ricky had descended on them with the news that she was going along. Gale was glad of the other girl's companionship for the Doctor was strangely silent.

The train was late and Gale found it hard to conceal her impatience. She was impatient for Phyllis' Aunt to arrive and yet she dreaded meeting her. The Adventure Girls had always feared the silent woman in the house on the hill. Now Gale did not fancy giving her the news about Phyllis. She would let Doctor Norcot handle the situation.

The woman that descended from the train was the same stern person Gale had known in Marchton. What change she had expected Gale did not know. She only felt now, suddenly, definitely, that Phyllis' case was lost before it was ever presented. This woman would not be charitable or generous.

The three had planned to take her to the one restaurant in the little village for luncheon. There, seated in a booth by themselves, Gale let Doctor Norcot tell Miss Fields all about Phyllis while she and Ricky listened.

The Doctor was eloquent in her praise of Phyllis. In the end she stressed particularly the need for the operation.

Gale forgot the dessert before her. With the silent Ricky she watched the sharp features of the woman opposite her. Miss Fields was regarding the plate before her with unwavering eyes. Not a flicker of emotion disturbed her features. Doctor Norcot glanced at Gale and smiled, a peculiarly baffled smile. Phyllis' chances now lay in Miss Fields' hands alone. Beneath the table Ricky's hand caught hold of Gale's.

Miss Fields glanced at her watch and rose. "It is almost time for my return train. Perhaps we should go."

The girls exchanged glances with the Doctor and followed Miss Fields from the restaurant. Silently they walked back to the station. The hour that Phyllis' Aunt proposed to spend in Briarhurst was up. Already her train was approaching.

"But aren't you going to see Phyllis?" Ricky demanded finally. She could be quiet no longer.

"What have you decided?" Gale asked breathlessly.

Miss Fields looked at Gale and actually smiled. It was a brief smile, and her eyes did not light with friendly warmth. Then she turned to the Doctor.

"I want to thank you, Doctor Norcot, for taking so much interest in Phyllis. I regret that I am not able to do what you suggest."

"You mean——" Gale began.

"You haven't the money?" Ricky put in brusquely. "But you are sending Phyl to college. You must have money!"

Miss Fields' eyes froze the garrulous Ricky with a single glance.

"My affairs are only my concern. My association with Phyllis concerns a promise I made many years ago. Believe me, I am truly sorry."

"But you must do something!" Gale said.

Phyllis' Aunt stepped onto the train. "It is impossible for me. Goodbye."

"A promise! Sorry!" Ricky stormed when the train had gone and they were on their way back to the campus. "She couldn't keep a promise or be sorry for anything!"

"I wonder what she meant?" Gale murmured. "Doctor Norcot," she said later, "are you going to tell Phyllis today?"

The Doctor took a deep breath. "She must know sometime. I'll go and see her this afternoon."

"I'll go with you," Gale said immediately.

"And I," Ricky added.

The Doctor smiled. "I would wait until tomorrow if I were you."

"She won't want to see us," Ricky agreed upon second thought.

"Wait until tomorrow when she will feel better. Then you must act as if nothing has happened—you must be perfectly natural. Don't make it any harder for her," the Doctor cautioned.

"You can count on us," Gale sighed. "When can she come back to the Omega Chi house?"

"In a few days," the Doctor promised. "She may feel better if she is with the girls."

"Then she won't have to leave college?" Ricky asked fearfully.

"No," the Doctor said, "not unless she wants to. She will be able to attend classes and get about but not without a cane or crutch—ever."

"There isn't any justice!" Ricky said savagely as she went up the Golden Stairs with Gale and entered the latter's room. "Why did such a thing have to happen to Phyl? Who——" she stopped in amazement and looked about the room. "What's happened?"

The room was topsy turvy. Bureau drawers were pulled out and the things tumbled about. The desks had been thoroughly searched. Even the closet door stood open and the girls could see the tumult within.

Gale smiled. "Someone was hunting for that note, I'll wager."

Ricky had been taken into the girls' confidence. Now she stared wide-eyed at Gale. "Did they find it do you suppose?"

"Hardly!" Gale pulled the note from her coat pocket. "Since I know someone else would like to have it, I keep it with me."

"Have you discovered the typewriter that wrote it?"

"No. The girls are still hunting," Gale laughed. "Every time they see a typewriter they run for it."

Ricky and Gale set things to rights and then Ricky departed to find Gloria. Gale went downstairs and over to the dormitory house to tell Valerie and the others about Phyllis. They might as well all know now.

She was still puzzling over Phyllis' Aunt's words. A promise? To whom? No promise was important enough to stop her aiding Phyllis now!

Miss Fields had been a mystery to the girls in Marchton ever since they knew her. They had always looked with awe upon the grey silent house and the woman who lived there. Through Phyllis they had glimpsed the life of Miss Fields— cold, always calm. Gale reminded herself that she had really been prepared for this. She had not thought in the very beginning that Miss Fields would have the money. Yet she had hoped against hope for Phyllis' sake. Now there was nothing to be done.

Over and over again the words recurred to Gale. Miss Fields' association with Phyllis concerned a promise she had made several years ago. But what sort of a promise? Gale, quite suddenly, had a brilliant idea. At first she had thought she must wait until the Christmas vacation or at least until she went home for Thanksgiving before she could question Miss Fields more closely, for question her she was going to! Certainly she was not going to consider the matter closed now! Gale was determined to do everything in her power to help Phyllis. She knew she could count on the other girls to feel the same. Gale was going to get to the bottom of Miss Fields' reserve! She determined to find out just what the woman meant. But Thanksgiving was several weeks away—Christmas even more so. She would write to David Kimball. He was a boy in Marchton who had been Phyllis' staunchest ally. He would help. He could set in motion the wheels of their action. While he studied law in Marchton he could aid Phyllis. She would write to David tonight!

Chapter XI

PHYLLIS

Phyllis sat by the window and looked over the campus. It was the last day of classes before Thanksgiving. Tomorrow the girls would be going home for the holiday. But she was going to stay right here. Her Thanksgiving dinner would be served here in her room as so many other meals lately had been. Oh, there would be other girls in the building, she would not be alone. But she would feel lonely nevertheless.

Gale was going home. Phyllis smiled reminiscently. Gale had been sweet these last weeks and so had the other girls. They had all been marvelously good to her—but that, to her, was worse than if they had quarreled and shouted at her. If only something would happen to break the even tenor of her days! If only the girls weren't always so sweet, so considerate! They felt sorry for her, she knew, and it irked her. She was going to classes again now, studying, but college life wasn't the same. There were no extra activities for her. She could not partake of the basketball games in which Carol and Janet starred. She could not join the dancing classes which claimed all Valerie's attention. She could not hope to ride in the spring riding classes to which Ricky and the others were looking forward so joyfully.

She threw her book at the opposite wall with such vigor that the book bounced back and landed on the floor with a dull thud. If only something would happen! She was sick of being pampered. If they would only treat her as they had before her accident. They argued with her then, scolded—anything! Anything but this eternal sweetness and light! She herself felt anything but sweet. She was tired of having to be courageous, always appearing to be cheerful! She wanted to let out some of the pent-up energy.

She looked down upon the campus. Gale and Valerie with Carol and Janet were coming toward the sorority house. They seemed to be in a hurry and kept glancing up at the window where she sat. She smiled ruefully. At last she had given them something to stir them. Now perhaps something would happen—at least, they wouldn't change her mind! Phyllis laid her cane on the floor beside her chair and turned to face the door. Sunshine Alley was about to have a bit of a thunderstorm.

"We won't stand for it!" Carol said the second the door opened.

Phyllis merely smiled.

"What do you mean by it anyway?" added Janet.

"Just what I said," Phyllis replied. "I am resigning as president of the Freshman class."

"But why? You must have a reason!" Valerie put in.

"I have a reason," Phyllis said stubbornly. "I can't go to all the class activities, I can't run around and be in everything that the president is supposed to—so I am resigning."

"We won't accept it," Gale said determinedly.

"You have to call a meeting of the class and it will be accepted. It has to be!" Phyllis said.

"But, Phyl," Janet pleaded, "we want you to be the president. All the girls feel the same."

"It wouldn't be fair to the class," Phyllis insisted. "A president is active—she has a lot to do. Well, I can't do it so I'm resigning. It is very simple."

"We won't let you," Carol said finally. "Val, you are secretary. Do something about it."

"I already have," Valerie said surprisingly. "I and the Vice President and the Treasurer."

"Well?" Phyllis said eagerly. "The officers agreed to accept my resignation, didn't they?"

"They did not," Valerie said. "We agreed, and posted a notice in the East Campus Dormitory to the effect, that you are still our president. Gale is president pro tem, and any one who disagrees must see one of us. How does that suit you?"

"You mean Gale is to act in the places where I can't?" Phyllis asked.

Valerie nodded.

"Then I'm president in name and Gale does the work," Phyllis said. "That isn't fair."

"I'll love it," Gale assured her bouncing on the bed. "That will give me authority. And will I use it!"

"That is what I'm afraid of," Carol grimaced. "See here, Miss President pro tem, don't think you can order me around."

Gale laughed. "I am going to try. Tonight there is a party here and you gals can come providing you go home now and let Phyllis rest."

"I don't want to rest," Phyllis put in fretfully. "Stay here and talk to me."

Carol looked from Gale to Phyllis.

"To go or not to go, that is the question!" misquoted Janet.

"Gale is so hospitable," laughed Carol.

"I don't know about the rest," Valerie said, "but I have to go. The Christmas entertainment given by the Freshman class is being planned and the secretary has a lot of work."

"While the president takes things easy," Phyllis said bitterly.

"Who is going to sing?" Janet asked.

"Yes," added Carol, "I heard the class is in need of a good contralto. Who is the star who is to sing in the chapel?"

Valerie shook her head. "Something else to keep me awake at night. I am on the committee to put the entertainment over and I haven't the faintest idea who we will choose."

"How about Phyl?" Gale asked.

"Phyl!" Janet echoed. "Of course! You've a fine voice, Phyl."

Phyllis laughed. "But I won't be in the entertainment!"

"All you have to do is sing," Carol seconded.

"But it is impossible," Phyllis said. "Me? Sing in the chapel? Don't be ridiculous."

"But——"

"I won't listen to another word," Phyllis said. "You don't know what you are asking."

"Phyl, you would——"

"No!" Phyllis almost shouted. "I would be scared to death."

Gale winked at Valerie. "She would be scared to death, girls," she murmured. "So that settles the question. Now will you go home? Go home and pack your things and get ready to leave tomorrow morning."

"We won't have time to pack tonight," added Janet. "See you tonight for the party," she added.

The early evening was already descending on the campus and Gale lighted the light.

"You didn't have to chase the girls home," Phyllis said peevishly.

Gale said nothing, merely seated herself at her desk and opened her French book. She did not try to concentrate her attention on the pages before her. She was acutely aware of Phyllis moving about. Gale longed to help Phyllis but she sat in her place not paying the slightest heed to the slow and difficult movements of her friend. Suddenly when Phyllis stumbled and would have fallen Gale sprang up and saved her.

"Let go!" Phyllis said indignantly. "I can make it by myself."

Instantly Gale's arms relaxed. She knew Phyllis must get used to the difficulties of her movements now but it was hard to sit by and do nothing. Gale turned away to her desk again. A few seconds later she felt Phyllis' hand on her shoulder.

"Sorry, I didn't mean to snap at you," Phyllis said.

"It is all right," Gale said.

"But it isn't all right," Phyllis insisted stormily. "I snap at you—I snap at all the girls. It is only because——"

"I know," Gale said. "But you mustn't think about things so much, Phyl. Something will be done. This may only be for a little while. We'll think of a way——"

"A way!" Phyllis murmured helplessly. "My Aunt was here, wasn't she, and refused to do anything? She was my only hope."

"How did you know?" Gale demanded sharply.

"Ricky," Phyllis said. "She said something that set me thinking. I asked her point blank and insisted on her telling me." She laughed a little. "Poor Ricky, she tried so hard not to let me know."

"We will do something, Phyl," Gale assured her friend more hopefully than she felt. "You've got to make the best of things for a little while."

"A little while!" Phyllis echoed. "It has been months!"

"Well," Gale laughed, "if you are looking for an argument with me you are going to be disappointed. I refuse to quarrel. I——"

"Gale!" Phyllis whispered frantically. "The window! There is a ladder being propped against it!"

Gale ran to the window and threw it open. "Someone is climbing up," she said smiling.

"Who?"

"I think you know," Gale laughed.

A dark head followed by broad shoulders hove above the window sill. A laughing voice spoke out of the November dusk.

"Hi, Phyl."

"David!" Phyllis cried. "David!"

"In person," he assured her.

"But how——"

"I have the Dean's permission to call on you properly tonight at eight," he said laughing, "but I couldn't wait. She would probably chase me out if she could see me now, though. I met Carol and Janet on the campus a few minutes ago and they very helpfully suggested this method. It is effective if startling."

"I'm going down for my dinner," Gale said and disappeared.

Gale had her dinner and then went out on the campus. She could see David on the ladder and Phyllis at the window. She waited in the darkness until she saw David descending the ladder. She joined him when he was safely on the ground.

"When did you get here, David?" she asked shaking hands.

"This afternoon," he replied. "I went immediately to the Dean's office. I didn't know whether I could see Phyllis or not. She is nice, your Dean."

"Staying in the village?" Gale asked.

"Yes. I'm going to stay until after Thanksgiving," he answered. "The Dean said I might entertain Phyllis while the girls are gone for the holiday."

"She needs someone," Gale said. "I'm glad you're here, David."

"I gathered that," he said seriously. "She seems pretty depressed."

"Did you see her Aunt?" Gale asked. "You know I wrote you what she had said and asked you to see her. Did you?"

David shook his head. "She hasn't been in Marchton since I received your letter. I went to the house and asked the woman who cooks for her when she expected Miss Fields back. She doesn't know."

Gale sighed. "It seems we are balked at every turn. I intend to find out what it is all about when I get back to Marchton. If not now, at Christmas."

"I'll try to keep Phyllis cheered up until you get back," David promised.

Gale returned to the sorority house then. She had to help Ricky set the stage for their party. Phyllis would see David again at eight o'clock while the other girls were upstairs. Gale would see that they had the living room to themselves for a long talk. She knew Ricky would aid her if there was any difficulty in engineering a serene night for Phyllis.

Chapter XII

FURTHER DEVELOPMENTS

Gale tramped through the snow feeling light-hearted and gay. Snow always seemed to have such a psychological effect upon her. Whether it was the lightness of it, or the brightness of the sun shining on the surface of the snow she did not know. At any rate she felt at ease with the world.

College had resumed at high speed for the short time between Thanksgiving and Christmas. Now it was but a week until the Christmas holidays. Gale felt joyfully elated. Last night she and Phyllis had carefully wrapped Christmas presents and hidden them in their trunks. There was a spirit of excitement in the air. The girls went about with mysterious bundles and smiles.

Even Phyllis seemed to be nearly back to her old cheerful spirits. Ever since Thanksgiving when David had appeared at the college Phyllis was happier, calmer. Gale was glad. She had had absolutely no success in Marchton. Miss Fields had not been at home. It had been as David said. No one knew where she had gone or when she was coming back.

Gale ran lightly up the steps and disappeared into the Dean's office. The Dean's secretary was absent so Gale knocked on the door to the inner sanctum where the Dean had her private office.

"Come in."

Gale opened the door and stepped within.

"Oh, Gale." The Dean looked up. She was just slipping into her coat. "Be seated. I want to mail this letter. It must get off immediately."

"I'll mail it for you," Gale offered.

"No, I'll drop it myself. It will only take a moment. Wait for me."

Gale looked about the empty office. There was a typewriter next to the Dean's desk. Her curiosity getting the better of her Gale inserted a sheet and typed a few words. It was not the smoothness or noiselessness of the machine that attracted her, but the letters themselves. The letters were even, in perfect alignment, all but the R. That was slightly raised. Gale could scarcely believe her eyes. She jerked the paper from the machine and brought the old mysterious note from her pocket. There was no question about it! The two had been written on the same machine! But it was impossible—incredible!

The Dean had not sent them that note, had she? Certainly not! But who then? Her secretary? Gale looked dubious. There was more in this situation than she had guessed. That she decided before—but now! How had this note been written on the Dean's typewriter? She put both sheets of paper into her pocket again as she heard footsteps in the outer office.

"Now, Gale, what is it?" The Dean removed her coat and seated herself behind her desk.

"Phyllis. She has decided she doesn't want to go home for Christmas. She would rather stay here. David, Mr. Kimball, wants to come to Briarhurst again and see Phyllis over the holidays." Gale drummed lightly on the space bar of the typewriter. "A nice typewriter, Dean. Just new?"

"Yes, my secretary bought it yesterday."

Yesterday! Gale added that to the storehouse of facts in her mind. Yesterday! Yet she was sure the mysterious note had been written on it months before! She scarcely heard the Dean's permission for David to come to Briarhurst as he had done on Thanksgiving, so busy was she turning over this new development.

Her business with the Dean concluded, Gale left. She had dinner with Janet and Carol at the East Campus Dormitory and after that they all went to the chapel to hear the Freshman's musical Christmas entertainment.

The organ was playing when the girls entered. The chapel was decorated with holly and poinsettias. In the corner a mammoth Christmas tree with the traditional white star at the top sent out a fragrance of spruce and Christmas cheer.

The girls sang carols and there were several solos. But the best liked soloist was a mystery. From the region of the organ, behind the holly and spruce display, came a girl's voice. The others listened spellbound. Such richness and expression! Every note was as clear as a bell. The music rang through the chapel and brought a new understanding and appreciation of Christmas to the listeners.

"Who is it?" Janet was simply bursting with curiosity.

"She is superb!" Gale echoed. "I never heard a voice like that."

Valerie was sitting beside them, the smile of sweet satisfaction on her face a mystery.

"You were on the committee, Val, who is it?" Carol coaxed.

"It is a secret," Valerie said. "But isn't she fine?"

"Wonderful," Gale agreed. "I wish Phyllis could hear her."

"Why didn't Phyllis come?" Madge whispered.

"She said she was too tired."

"Shshshsh," Janet warned as the soloist began again. "I could listen to her for hours. Is she somebody from the college, Val?"

"Of course," Valerie nodded.

"Oh, if I only had a voice like that!" Carol sighed.

"Then you would get some place," Janet agreed. "That girl will be famous."

Valerie smiled to herself.

When the quiet, musical evening was over the girls voted it a huge success. They doubted if even the play on the next night could hold them as enthralled. The Juniors and Seniors who had been present were quite as enthusiastic.

"We want that singer in the Glee Club," Adele Stevens said firmly. She was the active president of the organization and she did not intend to miss adding such a fine voice to the group.

"I don't know," Valerie said dubiously. "We had a hard time persuading her to sing tonight."

"But why didn't she come out from behind the shrubbery?" Carol complained. "We want to know what she looks like."

"Shrubbery!" Janet said horrified. "Carol Carter! To call our decorations that after the time we had arranging them!"

"Sorry," Carol laughed. "Who put the star on the top of the tree?"

"Madge," Janet giggled, "and she almost pulled the tree over a half dozen times."

The girls paused in front of the sorority house.

"Perhaps we shouldn't come in if Phyllis is tired," Janet said.

"Come along," Valerie said lightly. "She can bear it this once. No one should be tired around Christmas time."

The girls trouped up the stairs singing as they went. They found Phyllis sitting at her desk, her cheeks flushed and eyes bright.

"Greetings, my little sugar plum," Carol said lavishly. "You don't know what you missed tonight."

"What?" Phyllis asked.

"A singer—and what a singer! Honestly, that girl could be the musical sensation of the year."

Valerie and Phyllis exchanged glances then they both started to laugh.

"What's so funny?" Janet demanded.

"Either you girls are awf'ly innocent or you haven't the brains I thought you had," Valerie said between laughs. "Don't you see? Phyllis was the singer. She was the soloist tonight."

"Phyllis!" Gale echoed.

Janet and Carol howled together: "And you never told us!"

"A fine pal you are!" Janet grumbled.

"I'm disgusted with you," added Carol. "Hiding a voice like that! We knew you were good—but never that good!"

"I didn't want to do it," Phyllis confessed. "But Valerie said I didn't have to appear before all of you. No one would know who I was. I thought it would be fun to surprise you."

"You certainly did," Carol declared. "So much so that Adele Stevens wants you in the Glee Club."

"Never more can you be the shrinking violet," Janet nodded. "Now you will blossom forth in notes of song and we shall see you never more. Ah, me, such is the price of fame."

"Wait a minute," Phyllis laughed. "I sang tonight but that was only because Val wouldn't give me a moment's peace, otherwise. I don't intend to join the Glee Club."

"It would be good for you," Gale said. "You've always liked music, Phyl."

Phyllis yawned. "But now I believe I would like bed better."

"Just a gentle hint," Carol chaffed. "It seems we are always getting put out of here."

"You shouldn't come at such late hours then," Phyllis said.

"Tell me," Janet said, "since you are surprising us, you aren't going to be Santa Claus in the play tomorrow night, are you?"

Phyllis giggled. "Hardly!"

"Of course not," Carol said indignantly. "She hasn't got a beard."

Gale opened the window. Voices drifted up on the night air. The sorority girls were just ending their sorority song.

"We link our hands in friendship,
The girls of Omega Chi."

"I hope we get elected to the sorority," Carol said. "Then perhaps we can move in here with you next term."

"We aren't even members," Gale reminded them. "We are here only on the recommendation of Miss Relso. If she hadn't written for us we would never have gotten rooms in Happiness House."

"If we aren't elected to the sorority in May we will have to move," Phyllis added.

"What's that?" Carol shrieked as she backed away from the window.

"What?"

"Two eyes—staring in at me out of the darkness," she pointed to the window. Phyllis and Gale laughed.

"Only an owl in the tree out there," Phyllis said. "He is often there at night."

"Why don't owls sleep at night?" Janet wanted to know. "Are they afraid to sleep in the dark?"

"And do deers ever blow their horns?" Carol questioned. "We better go to our own domicile," she added at the dark glances from her friends. "Au revoir, ma chérie," she murmured in her very best French.

From the window Gale and Phyllis watched the girls disappear in the direction of the East Campus Dormitory.

"You were wonderful tonight, Phyl," Gale declared earnestly. "And were we surprised! When did you decide to sing?"

"Valerie talked me into it," Phyllis laughed. "She said I should do something like that—so I would have a part in the Christmas celebration I really enjoyed it."

"Phyllis—are you sure you won't go home with me for Christmas?" Gale asked sitting on the bed beside Phyllis. "I would love to have you."

Phyllis shook her head. "No. I can't go to my Aunt's place—I could but I don't want to, so I'll stay here. Besides," she said, eyes twinkling, "David is coming. I won't be lonesome."

"That reminds me," Gale said, "I meant to tell the other girls, too. Tonight when I went to the Dean's office I had to wait a while for her. While I was waiting I tried her typewriter. Guess what I discovered!"

"What?"

"Our mysterious note was typed on her machine. What do you deduct from that? I didn't tell her because I wanted to think about it for a while. It seems strange."

"Her own typewriter!" Phyllis echoed.

"And she told me she bought the typewriter only yesterday!"

"It can't be," Phyllis frowned. "There is something wrong someplace. Whom did she buy the typewriter from?"

"She said her secretary bought it," Gale said slowly. "I wonder if her secretary is everything she should be?"

"Certainly she wouldn't eat candy she knew was poisoned," Phyllis said. "She was sick from it, remember."

"If it was poisoned." Gale ran slim fingers through her hair. "The whole thing is beyond me. I'm not such a master mind after all."

"We will let it wait until after Christmas," Phyllis said.

The girls were forced to do that. Nothing more could be discovered at present and there was too much excitement with the holidays to bother about it.

Chapter XIII

STARTLING NEWS

Gale opened one eye and peered at the clock. The next instant she was up and hurriedly dashing through her usually methodical routine of dressing. It was Christmas morning. She was home with her parents and Brent was here! Last night had been the most glorious Christmas Eve she had ever experienced. The Adventure Girls, with the exception of Phyllis of course, and Brent and the other boys had gone carolling. After that there had been sandwiches and hot chocolate in the Howard living room where they could admire the big Christmas tree. Then, when the others had gone, a long intimate talk with Brent, learning all about his work in Washington and telling him all about her college life.

Now she pictured Brent waiting downstairs and, important enough too, a lot of mysterious packages beneath the Christmas tree just waiting to be opened. With a final approving look at the laughing, gray-eyed girl in the mirror, Gale dashed out into the hallway. With a cheer she slid down the banister and landed right in Brent's arms.

"Merry Christmas!" she said gaily.

"Merry Christmas yourself. Your Dad and I had about decided you were going to sleep all day." He tucked her arm within his. "How about some breakfast? I'm famished!"

"Before we open our presents?" she demanded. "I should say not!"

Saint Nicholas had been more than generous in his gifts to Gale and the others. After a long time spent examining and exclaiming over what the boxes disclosed they went to church. Then a long walk home through the brilliant sunlight and a most satisfying dinner.

"You know," Gale confessed to Brent, "I keep thinking about Phyllis. I told you what her Aunt said that day, didn't I? Let's go see Miss Fields. I want to ask her what she meant—if she is home."

"As you say," Brent agreed.

The two walked up the long hill arm in arm. The air was cold and invigorating. Gale felt she must burst with personal happiness yet she found time to think of Phyllis and wish, as often before, that there was something she could do.

The house on the hill was gray and silent, just as she had pictured it when she was at Briarhurst. The shutters were closed on most of the windows and there was a forlorn, deserted look about the place.

"I think you will be disappointed," Brent said. "It looks as though it is closed up for the winter."

"I hope she is here," Gale said.

Brent used the old iron knocker vigorously. They could hear the sound echo in the room beyond. They waited several minutes before Brent knocked again. To their surprise the door was opened almost immediately and by Miss Fields herself.

"H-Hello," Gale began uncertainly. "I want to talk to you, Miss Fields."

"I'm sorry, I'm busy," the woman said.

"I've got to talk to you!" Gale insisted. "About Phyllis."

Grudgingly the woman opened the door farther and Gale took advantage of it to slip within. Brent followed and then there was nothing for Miss Fields to do but lead the way into the cold, dark front room.

Gale shivered as she sat on the edge of an old-fashioned stuffed sofa beside Brent. This was a terrible place, so cold and damp and dark. She wagered no sunlight had been inside the house since Miss Fields took residence there, and that was years and years. Brent reached over and took Gale's hand in his warm grasp. It seemed to be what she needed.

"Well?" Miss Fields' voice was frigid and she sat stiffly in her chair.

"I—that is——" Gale began lamely. "We, the girls, are anxious to help Phyllis all we can. We can't do it without your aid."

"Well?" Miss Fields repeated.

"We want to know why you won't help," Gale said quickly.

Miss Fields grew even more frigid if that were possible. She regarded Gale with the utmost disdain and Gale was glad of Brent's presence. She felt she would have withered away under such a glare if she had been alone.

"I told you that day at Briarhurst it was impossible," she said.

"I know," Gale agreed, "but we want to know why. You must think we are impertinent, but you see we think an awful lot of Phyllis. Something must be done."

"It will do you no good to question me," Miss Fields returned. "If that is all I will wish you good day."

"Wait!" Gale cried when the woman would have left them.

"You have no right to make Phyllis suffer because of a promise you made years ago. She can be cured and you can help! There is no promise important enough to stop that!"

A cool glance was all the reply she got.

"You've got to help Phyllis," Gale insisted doggedly. She took a deep breath and looked at the woman almost pityingly. "I had no idea anyone could be so hard-hearted—so unfeeling! No wonder Phyllis hates you!"

To the utter amazement and consternation of Gale and Brent, Phyllis' Aunt sank into a chair and covered her face with her hands.

"I know she hates me," Miss Fields said in a dry whisper, "but I'd do anything for her."

Gale looked at Brent and he looked at her. Was she hearing aright? Was this the cold stern woman whom they had always accused of having no feeling whatever—of being cruel to Phyllis? It seemed Gale's words had released a spring of words that had been harbored too long.

"I've raised Phyllis since she was two years old. I've never meant to be cruel but I've been afraid I would lose her," Miss Fields continued staring at the floor. "I was jealous and afraid of the friends she made—it seemed to take a part of her away from me. I wanted to know what she was doing—I wanted her to love me."

Gale refrained from commenting on the fact that Miss Fields had taken a mighty strange manner of showing her love for Phyllis. She listened incredibly to the story of this strange lonely woman who had raised Phyllis. It was a cry of a heart which had at last broken through the cast of steel and ice which had so long encased it. It was hard to believe that Miss Fields really possessed a genuine affection for Phyllis. But, Gale admitted slowly to herself, it might be possible for one, such as Miss Fields, to want to have Phyllis' affection solely for herself, to be jealous of the girl's outside activities and friends because it meant a branch of life in which she could not share. She had overlooked, in her blind striving for all of Phyllis' companionship, the girl's craving for friends her own age and the other interests of younger people.

"I realize what this—this accident has meant to her," Miss Fields assured them. "I would help—I've tried to think of a way—but I can't. My hands are tied."

Brent leaned forward and spoke for the first time.

"Phyllis is not really your niece, is she, Miss Fields?"

Gale looked at him in surprise. This was a new angle! Phyllis not really Miss Fields' niece? What did he mean?

Miss Fields stared at Brent. Her eyes had the hunted look of an animal caught in a trap.

"What do you mean?" she asked fearfully.

"You might as well tell us everything," Brent pursued kindly. "We only want to help straighten matters out. Phyllis isn't really your niece, is she?" he insisted.

Miss Fields looked down at her hands clasped together tightly in her lap. Finally she raised her head.

"No," she said.

"I thought so," Brent murmured. "You had better tell us about everything. All about what happened years ago——"

Miss Fields fixed her eyes on the opposite wall and started to speak. It was as if she had forgotten the young people to whom she was talking, merely repeating a story that had been lodged in her mind for years.

"Years ago I was secretary to a Doctor. He had a wife and a little girl. One day his wife was killed in a bad railroad accident. Before she died she made me promise to stay with Phyllis. The Doctor was heart-broken and partly to forget, partly to further his ambition, he decided to go to Europe to study surgery. He left his little girl with me and enough money to keep her until he should return and longer."

"Didn't he ever return?" Gale asked anxiously.

"I lived in his house with Phyllis for two years. Then one day I received a wire that he was returning. I thought of all sorts of things—that I might be discharged—I might never see Phyllis again. I was lonely—I had no family, and I had grown to love the little girl like my own daughter." She looked sadly at Gale. "I brought Phyllis here. I've hidden her all these years——"

"Her father?" Gale asked.

Miss Fields bowed her head. "He returned to Europe after a few years—when he didn't find us. I've always been afraid someone would discover who she was —that is why I didn't want Phyllis to make friends—I was afraid. Now you know everything—what do you propose to do?"

Gale looked speechlessly at Brent. Her head was whirling with the new discovery. What a story had been here in their midst! Phyllis was the heroine of a story as incredible and fantastic as any fiction. What were they to do first?

"Who is her father?" Brent asked.

Miss Fields looked at him silently for a long moment. "Doctor Philip Elton," she said finally.

"The famous surgeon?" Brent echoed in surprise.

Miss Fields nodded. "But no one knows where he is. When I learned Phyllis needed money for an operation I tried to get in touch with him. I was willing then to let him know about Phyllis because I couldn't help her any more—but he could. It was impossible. He is somewhere in Europe."

"We've got to find him," Gale said excitedly. "Think what it means to Phyl——"

Brent rose. "We will start a search immediately. When he is found he can decide what is to be done," he told Miss Fields.

Gale and Brent went out into the sunshine leaving the woman sitting alone in the cold forlorn house.

"To think of all that being hidden for years and years," she murmured as they walked toward her home. "Because Miss Fields was so selfish. She didn't think what it might mean to Phyllis——"

"I'll start the search for Doctor Elton," Brent planned. "I suppose David will want to help when he returns."

"Do you think we should tell Phyllis now?" Gale asked. "Or do you think it would be better to wait until her father is found?"

"Perhaps it would be wiser to wait a little while," Brent agreed.

They reached Gale's home and entered the warm living room.

"Why don't you take your overcoat off?" Gale asked. "You are going to stay a while, aren't you?" she continued humorously.

Brent shook his head. "No. I'm flying back to Washington this afternoon."

"Brent!" she wailed. "You didn't tell me."

"I wanted it to be the happiest sort of Christmas," he replied. "Some day you will be going with me."

"Some day," she agreed.

When Brent had gone Gale curled up in the corner of the divan and watched the flames of the fire in the fireplace. She let her dreams run rampant. Some day she would be flying to Washington with Brent. She remembered what a thrill it had been flying to Canada with him last year. She remembered, too, the night of the Senior Prom when she and Brent had strolled in the garden.

But even over-riding all her rosy dreams was the astounding news she had heard about Phyllis that afternoon. It was like a fantastic fairy story. To think that Phyllis was the daughter of a famous surgeon, really a wealthy girl who had been hidden away in this small town all these years by a strange, selfish woman who claimed affection for the girl. Think what it must have meant to Phyllis' father—to return to his home to find the woman, whom he had entrusted with the care of his little girl, had disappeared taking his daughter with her. It must have been heart-breaking! But think what a reunion there would be when they met now—after all these years! How would Phyllis receive the news?

Gale pictured all sorts of ways to bring Phyllis and her father together yet the one which actually was to happen was even more dramatic.

Gale went to the telephone and put a long distance call through to Briarhurst. A few minutes later she heard Phyllis' voice.

"Merry Christmas!" Gale said gaily. "How are you? What did you do with yourself?"

"David hired a sleigh drawn by two horses and we had a long ride in the country," Phyllis said happily. "It was glorious."

They talked for a few moments and then Gale hung up, feeling satisfied that Phyllis had really enjoyed her Christmas after all. She had said nothing of her interview with Miss Fields, that would come later. Gale even doubted if she would tell the other Adventure Girls yet. It would be a secret between herself and Brent and David until Doctor Elton was found and could be produced.

She went back to her position before the fire. In ten days she would be going back to college. Then to pick up the threads of mystery concerning the Dean. This would be the spring term. Her riding lessons would start and she was anxious for them. Her only regret was that Phyllis would not be able to join her. Perhaps if her father was found and there was an operation performed Phyllis would eventually be as active as she had been. But not now!

Gale opened a book and nibbled on a chocolate caramel. She was perfectly content with her present position. A book was always a treasured companion to her. She could find much delight in following the adventures of a printed hero and heroine. Their adventures were always more dangerous, more glamorous than events in real life.

But alas, her composure and peace were not to last. There arose a loud clatter outside and the doorbell pealed long and loudly. Gale resignedly, smilingly, closed her book. Only the Adventure Girls would make so much noise.

Chapter XIV

DISCOVERED

"Look!" Carol pirouetted gracefully for the benefit of her friends.

"I'm speechless," Janet said appreciatively.

"Wait until I get my sun glasses," pleaded Phyllis. "I'm dazzled."

Carol was arrayed in the scarlet lounging pajamas she had received for a Christmas present. The Adventure Girls were all gathered in her and Janet's room viewing the display with mingled exclamations.

"And wait——" Carol murmured diving into the closet.

"More to come," Madge said shaking her head. "If it is as terrific as those pajamas, don't show it to me. My nerves won't stand it."

"My riding habit," Carol said proudly.

Janet laughed. "All you need now is the horse."

"I've heard they have a merry-go-round in the next village park," Valerie put in. "Perhaps they would let you practice there."

Carol made a little face at her. "Just the same, I am all prepared."

"What time is it?" Phyllis asked suddenly. "Heavens! I have to go. I promised Adele to go with her to the Glee Club meeting this afternoon."

"Ah, our singer is blossoming out," Janet said gleefully. "What did I tell you!"

"I'll go with you," Gale said. "I have to see Professor Lukens about our Chemistry assignment tomorrow."

The two girls went down to the campus. Gale saw Phyllis safely to the Glee Club meeting before she went on to the Chemistry Hall. The corridors and rooms were for the most part empty. She went to the classroom where the Professor often spent his afternoons going over papers. He was not there so Gale went on to the laboratory.

At the door she drew back hastily into the corridor. Someone was in the room but it was not the Professor. It was Miss Horton, the Dean's secretary, and the girl was fussing with the lock on the cabinet where the experimental materials were kept. Gale watched her cautiously through a crack in the door. The glass doors were suddenly opened. A small glass vial found its way from the closet into the pocket of the girl's coat.

Gale turned and fled down the hall. Outside she waited. Miss Horton came out. With a glance about she hurried down the steps and set off in the direction of the Dean's office. Gale followed, hurrying her steps to keep the girl in sight. At the corner of the building Gale bumped into Valerie.

"Going to a fire?" Valerie asked. "Say, Gale, do you know where I can find ____"

"Can't stop now," Gale said. "Val, something is going to happen. Find Doctor Norcot. Bring her to the Dean's office right away. Hurry!" Gale urged when Valerie hesitated.

Valerie broke into a run. Gale hurried on her way. Miss Horton was disappearing into the building. Gale followed and it was not until she was in the building that she realized she had no definite idea at all why she was so alarmed. True, it was strange that Miss Horton should break into the Chemistry cabinet and take something—Gale wasn't sure what. Could it have been Miss Horton who hurled that acid out the window at the Dean so many weeks ago? Could it have been Miss Horton who wrote that mysterious note to the girls? Could she have cut the rope to set Dean Travis' canoe afloat?

Yes, all those things were quite possible. But what was she up to now? There were a lot of things in that Chemistry cabinet—things which in the wrong hands could cause a lot of damage.

On tiptoe Gale approached the door to the outer office. Miss Horton was stirring a white liquid in a glass. On her desk was the discarded vial from the Chemistry laboratory—empty! The contents had been put into the glass with something else. Gale watched the silent actions of the girl within the room. Miss Horton was nervous, erratic, in her movements. She appeared slightly crazed with an inner obsession. The telephone rang, the bell startling both Gale and the girl inside.

Miss Horton stared at the instrument for a moment then picked up the receiver. She sank into her desk chair.

"Sarah! Why did you call? Of course I'm all right. Don't worry. Do you understand? Don't worry! And Sarah—you will be Dean of Briarhurst someday."

With those words Miss Horton replaced the receiver. She looked about the room and stood up. Grasping the glass again she walked toward the Dean's office. She opened the door and spoke. Gale could clearly hear her words.

"This will help your headache, Dean Travis."

Gale lost no time. She dashed wildly into the office, knocking the glass from the Dean's upraised hand, thinking at the same time what would happen if she was wrong in her suspicions!

"Don't drink it!" she cried.

The glass crashed to the floor and made a dark stain on the carpet. Miss Horton gazed at Gale in horror, shrinking toward the door.

"Gale! What does this mean?" the Dean gasped.

"It means Miss Horton broke into the Chemistry laboratory and took a vial—poison probably. She mixed it in that glass," Gale continued accusingly.

"Is this true?" the Dean asked, looking from Gale to her now sobbing secretary.

The girl did not answer. Doctor Norcot and Valerie appeared in the doorway.

"What is going on?" the Doctor demanded breathlessly. She held up the empty vial which had been on the secretary's desk. "Whom does this belong to?"

"Gale——" Valerie said in mystification.

"It is all right now," Gale said, "Miss Horton almost poisoned the Dean. I followed her here from the Chemistry laboratory."

"Yes, I meant to poison her," Miss Horton said desperately, hysterically. "If it hadn't been for her my sister would be Dean of Briarhurst. She worked years to have the position, she studied in Europe, everything to fit herself for this. Then you came along," the girl said to Dean Travis, "and were appointed. It nearly broke my sister's heart."

"You thought if you could get rid of me your sister would still have a chance," Dean Travis said slowly. "Is that it?"

"Yes. Now I've failed. You might as well know, I took the money from your safe, too. I meant to put it back—but I couldn't right away. Now you will probably send me to prison."

The Dean smiled in sympathetic understanding. "No, but if you return the money, pack your things and leave tonight, we will forget the whole incident."

"Now," Valerie pounced upon Gale when they were outside. "Tell me what happened? It was all a mystery to me yet you seemed to know all about things."

"Simple," Gale grinned. "Miss Horton's sister wanted to be Dean at the same time as Dean Travis. You know who won. Miss Horton evidently sought revenge for her sister. She was doing these things to frighten Dean Travis into leaving. Once she left, Miss Horton's sister stood a good chance of being appointed in her place."

"But Dean Travis didn't scare so easily, is that it?" Valerie asked.

"Right," Gale agreed.

"So Miss Horton was going to murder the Dean," Valerie shivered. "How horrible!"

"She didn't really know what she was doing," Gale said.

"And the Dean forgave her as if it were nothing at all," Valerie said. "Attempted murder is a criminal offense."

"Miss Horton was too scared to ever do anything like it again," Gale said. "There was no use punishing her farther. After all, no harm was actually done."

"You forget the note and the mysterious man that night back of the Chemistry Hall," Valerie reminded her. "And what of Phyl's accident? Did someone push the lumber that day?"

"That we will probably never know—about the man I mean," Gale said. "She must have had someone with her. But I think she wrote the note. As for the lumber that caught Phyllis, I believe that really was an accident."

"Will the girls be surprised!" Valerie said. "Anyway, I'm glad I was in at the finish."

The girls were gathered in the living room of the sorority house. One of the Seniors had a small radio and she was fussing with it while the rest listened and idled away the time until dinner. Just as Gale entered and joined Phyllis and Ricky a voice from the radio proclaimed:

"Flash! An unconfirmed report has just been received that Doctor Philip Elton, the world renowned surgeon, is lost in the jungles of Brazil. Doctor Elton sailed from Liverpool, England, a month ago for a vacation cruise on his yacht, the *Tornado*."

"Some fun," Ricky commented. "I've heard all sorts of things about those jungles."

"Is he any relation to you?" Valerie asked of Phyllis smilingly. "Same name."

Gale held her breath until Phyllis had replied.

"Not that I know of," Phyllis laughed. "No relation of mine is fortunate enough to own a yacht."

Gale moved away. If she stayed with the girls another minute she would tell them the truth or burst!

"Hi, Gale!" A voice called. "Telephone!"

Gale shut the door to the small closet-like room which the girls had converted into a telephone booth.

"Hello? Yes."

It was Brent.

"Oh, Brent, I just heard the news about Doctor Elton. Phyllis heard it, too, and she doesn't suspect a thing."

"I called to tell you," Brent said. "David and I are flying down tonight. The South American government is sending out a searching party and we want to help."

"Take care," Gale pleaded. "The jungle is so dangerous."

"Who was it?" Ricky demanded, when Gale emerged.

Luckily the dinner summons saved Gale the necessity of an explanation. After dinner the girls retreated to their rooms to devote much needed time to their studies.

Gale looked up from her books to Phyllis. Phyllis was bent over a mathematics problem; her cane lay beside her chair and she looked very tired.

"Do you ever hear from Miss Fields, Phyllis?" Gale asked suddenly.

Phyllis looked up in surprise. "She sends me a monthly allowance. That is all, why?"

"I wondered. Did you always live with her, Phyl?" Gale continued slowly.

"I can't remember anyone else," Phyllis said. "Very faintly I recall a big house and a dog. We used to have grand times together. But I never had a dog in Marchton," she said, "so perhaps it is all a dream."

"Is Miss Fields your mother's or your father's sister?" Gale asked next. She knew the woman was neither, but she wanted to have Phyllis' thought on the subject.

Phyllis twirled her pencil between her fingers. "Perhaps you will think I'm funny, but sometimes I think she isn't even my Aunt."

"Why?" Gale asked intently.

Phyllis shrugged her shoulders. "I can't explain it. The feeling is just there. She never speaks about any of those things."

"Hmmm," Gale said.

"But this isn't getting my mathematics done," Phyllis sighed.

"Nor my Latin," Gale agreed.

The girls resumed their studies, but Gale's mind insisted on wandering off to picture an airplane bearing two young men toward South America. David and Brent were off to aid in the search for the famous surgeon—Phyllis' father! What if the Doctor wasn't found? Gale looked across at Phyllis. Practically all of Phyllis' future hinged on the news announcement they had heard downstairs and the girl did not know it!

"What are you going to do after college, Phyl?" Gale asked dreamily.

Phyllis laughed. "What's the matter, isn't the Latin interesting?"

"Terribly," Gale smiled. "But what are you?"

"I haven't the faintest idea," Phyllis confessed.

"Neither have I," Gale admitted, "unless it is to be a doctor. Anyway, you can go back to your mathematics." She turned her attention to her book again, but she couldn't concentrate on it. She wandered out of their room and downstairs. She found the Senior still at her radio listening to a popular comedian.

"Any more news flashes?" she asked.

"Nope."

Gale went back upstairs. She was restless. She wished she was with Brent and David. It was hard to wait for news. It was so much better to be in the center of the activity. But now it was doubly hard for her because she was the only one here who knew about Phyllis' father. If there was only someone she could talk it over with! But it was to be a secret and she would keep it. Still, sometimes she felt she must tell Phyllis that things would be brighter for her.

For days Gale's suspense continued. She attended classes, basketball games, club meetings, and every afternoon walked to the little village for an evening paper. There was very little news printed about Doctor Elton and his trip into the Brazilian jungle. Neither did Gale receive any word from Brent. She had not heard a thing since the night he telephoned her. Now she had an additional worry. Not only was she concerned about Doctor Elton, but more so about Brent's safety.

Day after day she scanned the newspapers, listened to news reports on the Seniors' radio and looked for a letter, but none of them yielded the news she hoped for. She tried to conceal all anxiety from Phyllis and the other Adventure Girls, but she wasn't very successful. They could not help but notice her sudden absorptions in newspapers and the radio. However, try as they would, they could not drag forth any explanation. Gale laughed all their questions aside.

Then one day came a thick letter from Brent. Gale received it in the living room and raced to the privacy of the girls' sanctum to read it. Lying on the bed, her chin propped on her hands, the letter against the pillow, Gale read it through once and then again. She rolled over on her back and stared at the ceiling.

Doctor Elton was found and Brent and David were flying him to Briarhurst. They would arrive on the seventeenth. This was already the fifteenth! They had told the Doctor Phyllis' story—also that she was his daughter. Brent said very little of what a revelation it must have been to the Doctor. She searched out a particular paragraph again.

"'Doctor Elton is willing to perform Phyllis' operation himself, but she is not to know until afterward that he is her father. Why he makes that reservation I do not know—unless it would be more of a trial and an ordeal for her knowing who he was. So, Gale, dear, it is up to you to get Phyllis ready to meet the Doctor. He wants to do things right away.'"

"Why so deep in thought?" Phyllis asked, when she entered.

"Phyllis——" Gale sat up. "Phyl, suppose you had the chance to have the operation that might make you all right again, would you go through with it?"

Phyllis grew a little pale.

"What do you mean?"

"Just that," Gale pursued. "Suppose the biggest doctor in the country said you had a chance—a very good chance, if your leg was operated on and reset, of walking again as you used to. Would you take it?"

"Would I take it?" Phyllis gasped incredulously. "Oh, Gale, need you ask? I'd take any sort of chance—even the slimmest."

"It means weeks again of convalescence—time in the hospital," Gale reminded her gently.

"But it would be worth it," Phyllis said. "Gale, tell me what you mean!"

Gale hugged Phyllis rapturously. "It means, Phyl, that Doctor Elton, the surgeon, is coming to Briarhurst to see you. He is going to perform it."

"When?"

"He arrives day after tomorrow."

"But the money?"

That momentarily stumped Gale.

"He is interested in you," Gale explained lamely. "Brent met him and was telling him about you and he——"

"An experiment, is that it?" Phyllis asked.

"Um—ah—sort of," Gale agreed. "But think what it will mean, Phyl! You'll even be back on the hockey team next year," she added gayly.

"Who will be on what hockey team?" Valerie asked, entering. "Greetings, Madam President and Madam Pro Tem. What did I interrupt?"

Phyllis breathlessly told her and went off happily to tell Ricky.

"How come, Gale?" Valerie asked, mystified. "To have Doctor Elton, THE Doctor Elton——"

"It is a long story," Gale said, swallowing a lump in her throat. "I'll tell you sometime, Val, but the main thing now is Phyllis—she is so happy."

"It is going to take a lot of courage to go through it all again," Val said. "I suppose there is no doubt about the success of the operation?"

"If Doctor Elton can't do it, it can't be done," Gale said firmly. "He is the best, Val. Besides that, he is her——"

"Her what?" Valerie asked interestedly.

"Nothing," Gale said hastily. "Here comes Phyl. Let's go tell Doctor Norcot and Dean Travis now," she proposed.

Chapter XV

PHYLLIS' STORY

Gale leaned her hot cheek against the coolness of the window pane.

The rain beating against the outside tinkled in her ear. She closed her eyes and swallowed a big yawn. From her position she could see the small town of Weston spread out before her. Lamps gleamed yellow gold, reflected on the shining wetness of the streets. Automobiles crawled past like bugs on a sheet of black paper.

"Do you suppose he will ever come out?" Gale asked wearily.

"It has been three hours," Valerie sighed. "It will scarcely be much longer."

David paced up and down the waiting room while Brent sprawled lazily in a leather chair and stared at the ceiling. The girls turned from the window and contemplated the room. They had come there early in the afternoon with Phyllis and Brent and David. At the hospital, for the first time they met Doctor Elton. He was a middle-aged man, good looking and dignified. Gale could see a strong resemblance between Phyllis and her father. The Doctor had immediately taken Phyllis away with him, being professionally kind, but not at all fatherish as Gale had remarked to Brent.

"That will come later," Brent told her.

The four of them had elected to wait until the operation was over. They had not seen Phyllis again. Now it was long past their dinner time and they were waiting for Doctor Elton to tell them of the success or failure of his work.

Gale argued with herself that there could be no thought of failure. Doctor Elton was skillful, the most marvelous surgeon of his kind in the world. But a little demon of pessimism reminded her that any operation could fail—no matter how skillful the physician. But not to Phyl! Not to Phyl! she repeated over and over. Phyllis certainly deserved a reward for all her bravery and courage.

The minutes dragged away into hours. The grayness of the world outside was seeping into the room. A nurse came in and quietly, efficiently lighted the lamps, straightened a group of magazines, and disappeared again.

"If somebody doesn't come to us soon," Valerie threatened, "I'm going hunting for Doctor Elton. Do you suppose he could have forgotten about us?"

Gale shook her head and turned again to the window. She did not relish the ride home to the college in the rain. They had been forced to bring Phyllis to Weston because it was the nearest town with a modern, sufficiently equipped hospital for Doctor Elton. Doctor Norcot was here, so Phyllis' father said. The girls had not seen her as yet, but Gale wished she would bring them some kind of news now.

"We better go out and get our dinner," Brent said finally. "We may have to wait quite a while yet."

"I couldn't eat anything," David said decisively, flinging himself into a chair, only to get up and walk restlessly about again.

"Nor I," Gale said.

She wondered if Doctor Elton proposed to tell Phyllis who he was tonight. Hardly, she decided later; this was scarcely an opportune moment. It would be a bit of a shock to find after all this time that Phyllis had a father, and that it should be Doctor Elton would be more stupendous still.

There were footsteps in the hall. All of them came to attention. Doctor Elton entered. His face was grave and pale. He looked more tired than anyone Gale had ever seen. It was as if all the cares in the world were on his shoulders. He seated himself in a chair and looked at them.

"Well?" David said impatiently.

"She will be well again," the Doctor pronounced. "Two months should see her back on her feet as before her accident. She is wonderfully brave," he murmured. "I have never seen such gay courage. I have just left her. She wants to see you," he added to the girls. "But only for a moment," he added warningly, "she must not be excited. The nurse will take you."

"I'll wait," Valerie said unselfishly. "Two of us might be too much."

Gale followed a white uniformed nurse down the narrow hall past numerous closed doors. At last the nurse halted and motioned for Gale to enter a corner room. Slowly Gale did so. Phyllis smiled at her.

"Hi!" her friend said faintly. "I came through, Gale."

"Splendidly!" Gale said. "Oh, darling, we're so glad for you. Gosh," she sniffed, "I'll cry in a minute. In that case I'll be put out."

"Do you suppose you can arrange it so I might see David for a few minutes?" Phyllis whispered.

Gale's eyes twinkled. "I'll try."

Twice a week after that for five weeks Gale made trips to the hospital to visit Phyllis. Sometimes Doctor Norcot drove her, sometimes she took a local bus, but on two occasions the Dean herself drove Gale.

One afternoon when Gale was making her visit alone Doctor Elton called her into the office before she saw Phyllis.

"So will you tell her, Gale?" the Doctor asked in conclusion. "I can't just rush in and say 'I'm your father.' It would be too dramatic and much too abrupt. Probably she won't believe it at first. I can hardly realize myself that I have a grown daughter."

At his frank smile Gale felt aglow with friendliness. The more she saw of Doctor Elton the more she liked him. She could see now where Phyllis got her capacity for making friends, her radiating smile and her sense of humor. Doctor Elton had spent all his time here in Weston, ever since the discovery of his daughter. But as yet Phyllis was ignorant of whom he really was.

"I'll tell her," Gale agreed. "But you had better be close at hand because I'm sure she will want to talk to you right away."

"I'll stand outside the door," he promised. He straightened his tie nervously. "Do you think she will like her father?" he asked with a smile.

"From what I have seen of you two together," Gale said, "she already likes you a lot."

Phyllis was in a chair by the window. The sun was streaming in. There were magazines and newspapers in profusion, but Phyllis was busy with none of these. She had a sketching board propped up before her and with charcoal was rapidly transferring the view from the window to the paper. The low buildings and the farther hillside upon which spring was already awakening trees and plants were pictured with exactly the right delicate shadows and lights.

Gale opened the door and closed it softly behind her. Phyllis did not hear her at all, so engrossed was she in the work at hand. Gale tiptoed across the room to look over Phyllis' shoulder.

"Splendid!" she commented gayly.

Phyllis was so startled the pencil dropped from her hand and rolled on the floor. Gale rescued it.

"You have been hiding things from me," Gale accused. "First a glorious voice and now real artistic ability. I am discovering that I hardly know you at all."

"Gale!" Phyllis welcomed her eagerly. "Sit down." She made room for Gale on the chaise-longue. "Did you hear? Did the Doctor tell you? I'm coming back to Briarhurst next week."

"You are!" Gale said joyfully. "I'm so glad."

"He thinks by the first of May I should be as good as new—no canes or crutches or anything."

"He is a wonderful man," Gale commented.

"Doctor Elton?" Phyllis murmured. "He is—he is—oh, words fail me," she laughed. "But I can never repay him for what he has done—or you either, for that matter."

"Me?" Gale gasped.

"You and David and Brent," Phyllis nodded. "I just know it was you who were responsible in bringing Doctor Elton to see me at all."

"It wasn't us alone. It was something much more important," Gale said slowly. She thought this was probably the best opportunity she would have to tell Phyllis about her father. "I've a story to tell you, Phyl—it is more interesting than a fairy story—and it is true. Remember that, it is true!"

"Reading fairy stories again, Gale?" Phyllis laughed. "Go ahead, I'm listening."

Gale took the sketching board and laid it on the floor, then she grasped both Phyllis' hands tightly in her own.

"It seems about nineteen years ago a little baby girl arrived at the home of a certain young doctor and his wife. The doctor was ambitious and wealthy. The three were supremely happy. But one day his wife was killed in a railroad accident. The doctor was broken-hearted and could really find peace of mind only in his work. He decided to go to Europe to study surgery—the height of his ambition. He entrusted his little girl to the care of a woman who for years had been his secretary. He gave her money and told her to look after the baby until he returned." Gale paused for breath. Phyllis was regarding her with steady, clear eyes.

"This woman grew to love the little girl," Gale continued, determined to be as charitable as possible to Miss Fields. "For two years the doctor remained in Europe making a name for himself—becoming famous. When he decided to come home the woman got panicky. She was afraid something would separate her from the little girl. She decided to run away and hide and take the girl with her. She found a small town and a lonely old house. The doctor returned to the United States, to his home, to find the woman and the child gone. No one knows exactly how long he searched before giving up in despair. Then he returned to Europe and his work again. Meanwhile, the woman and the girl remained hidden. The girl grew up into a sweet young lady and went away to college."

"Gale—what are you saying?" Phyllis whispered faintly.

"Don't you see, dear?" Gale asked gently. "You're the little girl—the doctor, your father, is Doctor Elton."

"Oh, no!" Phyllis said. "Gale, it can't be true—if you are teasing——"

"But it is true," Gale insisted smilingly. "I know it sounds fantastic but such things can happen. It has happened. Your Dad is here, Phyl, and he is never going to let you out of his sight again. He is waiting outside———"

"Bring him in," Phyllis said quickly. "Oh, please, Gale———"

"I won't bring him," Gale said, "I'll send him. I'm off to school again but I'll be back on Thursday."

Gale softly closed the door upon Phyllis and Doctor Elton. Smiling she went out into the sunshine and boarded the bus. She felt all vivid with joy herself to think that she had been able to help a little in giving Phyllis her new happiness—for there was no doubt that Phyllis was happy. Her eyes and face had told Gale that much.

Gale scarcely felt the bruises she acquired while being bounced around in the bus en route to Briarhurst. She was in a rosy dream-world where magical wishes and lovely thoughts came true. She descended in the little college town and walked up to the college still in blissful joyland. She found Carol and Janet and Valerie standing before the sorority house arguing.

"We are not going to tell her now and spoil everything!" Carol said conclusively.

"Tell who what?" Gale wanted to know.

"You know we have been saving the news of our equestrienne ability as a secret for Ricky. Being western born and bred she thinks she is the only one here who knows anything about a horse," explained Carol.

"I want to tell her about our summer in Arizona when we learned to ride like Indians," Janet put in. "She teased me unmercifully this afternoon. Told me tomorrow in our first riding class I wouldn't know one side of the horse from the other. I won't stand for it!"

"But it will only be for a few hours now," Valerie soothed her. "Imagine her surprise tomorrow when we calmly jump into the saddle and gallop off."

"Where have you been?" Carol asked Gale. "To see Phyl? How is she? I'm going with you on Thursday."

"She is on top of the world," Gale said happily. "All taken up with the discovery of her father."

"Ricky said———" Janet was continuing with her original theme when the import of Gale's words was borne in upon her. "Phyl is all taken up with what?" she asked.

"Yes, why don't you speak distinctly?" Carol added laughingly. "I almost thought you said something about Phyl's father."

"I did," Gale acknowledged calmly.

"But she hasn't———" Valerie began. "Wait a minute! Gale Howard! Have you been doing detective work on something unbeknownst to us?"

"It is a long story, gals," Gale said. "Come up to my room and I will unfold a tale that will make you throw away your latest detective novel for lack of interest."

Comfortably ensconced on her bed beside Valerie, while Carol and Janet hovered at comfortable if ungraceful angles on Phyllis' cot, Gale told them the story she had earlier unfolded to Phyllis. The girls were as astounded and as sceptical as Phyllis at first had been. However, they were all glad things had turned out so happily and profitably for Phyllis.

"Imagine," Carol said dreamily, "he gets lost in the jungles of Brazil and comes home to meet his daughter whom he hasn't seen for nigh onto eighteen years."

"He hasn't been lost in the jungle all these years," Janet corrected her friend.

"No," Carol admitted, "but isn't it wonderful?" she repeated. "Do you suppose," she continued hopefully, "he would lend us his yacht to go cruising this summer?"

"And get ourselves lost in the jungle as he did?" put in Janet. "No thanks! I have no desire to get eaten by a ferocious tiger."

"I just mentioned it," Carol said soothingly. "Besides, he wasn't eaten by a tiger."

"It was only a matter of time," Janet said knowingly. "He probably would have been eventually."

"Who knows," Carol said argumentatively, "perhaps he would have eaten the tiger."

"Oh, dry up!" Valerie said explosively. "When is Phyllis coming back to school, Gale?"

"Next week," Gale replied. "She won't be able to start classes right away and she will have to use crutches for two weeks or so, but the doctor thinks by the first of May she will be as fit as a fiddle."

"Coming back next week?" Carol sat up in inspiration. "We'll give her a surprise party."

"Fine," Janet agreed. "But there is one surprise I am more interested in right now—the one we are going to give Ricky tomorrow."

A week ago horses had arrived for the students. The girls had all inspected the ten mounts and each privately had her own decided upon. Surprisingly there were not many girls who were interested in the classes. A lot of them, especially the upper classmen, already were horsewomen or had their rosters so full they could not find time for any more after-hour activities. Not so the Adventure Girls, however. They were fully determined to ride as were Gloria and Ricky. The Adventure Girls had ridden a lot the summer they spent in Arizona. They could stick in the saddle of their mount at no matter how fast a pace on a flat stretch of road. At hurdles is where they encountered their difficulties and this is what they wanted to learn. They wanted to learn to take fences and broad jumps as easily as the riding instructor. It promised lots of fun as well as healthful exercise.

Chapter XVI

THE FIRST LESSON

"Now don't be frightened when the horse looks at you," Ricky advised Janet patronizingly as the five Adventure Girls with Ricky and Gloria walked to the new stables to meet the other two members of the class and their instructor.

"The horse will probably be frightened when Janet looks at it," Carol giggled shamelessly.

Janet favored them both with a look of utter disgust and settled her hat at a more rakish angle.

At the stables the girls found the two grooms with saddled mounts ready and waiting. Their instructor was already mounted. Several upper classmen had come down to watch the Freshmen get their first instructions. Among them was Marcia Marlette and Gale thanked her lucky stars that she knew something about riding. She would not look foolish before Marcia. The other two members of the class arrived and the girls took the reins of their mounts.

"Just watch me," Ricky whispered to Janet. "I'll show you how to mount."

Janet murmured something under her breath which Ricky innocently did not hear. Ricky swung into the saddle with the easy familiarity of being used to horses. Janet followed suit.

"Excellent!" Ricky applauded. "It almost looked as though you had done it before."

"I'm crazy about the merry-go-round," Janet explained, coughing away a giggle. "What do we do now?"

"Get the correct hold on the reins," Ricky instructed.

With the most guileless of expressions Carol and Janet, especially, went through the pantomimes of beginners. The upper classmen spectators were getting a lot of enjoyment out of the scene.

The horses were spirited mounts but easily handled by the girls. At last the instructions were beginning to pall upon Carol and Janet. They didn't like the leisurely pace they were forced to maintain for the class as a unit. When they came to an open stretch in the road Carol and Janet urged their horses alongside the instructor. They talked in low tones for several minutes; finally she nodded smilingly.

"Yipee!" Janet cheered. "Now, Ricky, we'll show you some riding!"

Side by side Janet and Carol spurred their horses on. The mounts, fresh and eager, galloped away sending up a cloud of dust in their wake. Ricky watched the two girls in amazement.

"Where did they learn to ride like that?" she gasped to Valerie.

"On the western plains," Valerie laughed. "We spent a summer there. Janet has been bursting to show you."

"Look at them go!" Gloria cried. "They really are good."

"On flat roads, yes," Madge smiled. "Let them come to a jump—and watch out."

"Let's catch them," Gale proposed.

An acquiescent nod from the instructor with a word of caution, and the Adventure Girls with Ricky were off in pursuit of their friends.

Carol and Janet were racing neck and neck down the road. They were trying recklessly to outrun one another. Their horses seemed to enter into the spirit of the occasion and raced ahead. The girls bent low in the saddles. They had not had so much fun since they were in Arizona.

"Race you to the old mill," Janet shouted.

"Be there ahead of you," retorted Carol.

Around a bend in the road ahead there was an old deserted water mill. Its water wheel was still now and the stream from which it had once secured current was a mere trickle of water through the woods. The girls had discovered the old mill on one of their jaunts about the countryside. Now Janet and Carol decided it would be a good spot at which to bring to a close their race.

"They must be heading for the old mill," Valerie cried to Gale as they followed their friends' trail of dust.

Ricky reined in her horse. "Girls, I, was there yesterday," she said excitedly. "There is a big oak tree down across the road. If they don't see it and jump——"

"Come on." Gale spurred her horse on anew.

She and the others could picture what might happen. Janet and Carol coming around the bend suddenly, totally unprepared for the tree across the road, might have a bad fall. If their horses did not make the jump there would most certainly be an accident. Even if their horses did clear the tree that did not say the girls would. They needed plenty of time to prepare for a jump and time to think of what to do. Horsemanship was not as instinctive with them yet as with Ricky. She could have cleared the jump without hesitating, but not so the other two

Freshmen.

Carol, her head down, whispering encouragingly to her horse, felt that she was having the most marvelous time of her college term. She had always loved thoroughbred horses. Inch by inch her mount pulled ahead of Janet. Gleefully she observed that at this rate she would win the race. They were rounding the bend of the road. Not much farther to go! Carol glanced over her shoulder at Janet. Her friend was gesticulating wildly and endeavoring to rein in her horse. Carol mistook her friend's gestures for enthusiasm and waved in return.

"Look out, Carol!" Janet shouted. "The tree! Jump!"

Janet saw her friend turn. Carol's horse was almost upon the huge trunk of an oak tree lying directly across the road. Carol stiffened, then bent forward on her horse's neck. Together, in marvelously graceful form, Carol's mount carried both himself and his rider over the fallen tree successfully.

However, Janet, surprised at the appearance of the tree and in her effort to warn Carol, had neglected to check her own mount. He raced ahead. Now it was too late to stop him.

The pursuing girls rounded the bend. Their horses raised a cloud of dust as they were brought to an abrupt halt by their riders.

"Janet!" Madge screamed.

The girls saw Janet's horse try to take the jump. He rose into the air but with an inexperienced rider his jump was not successful. His hind feet caught on the trunk, throwing both him and his rider heavily to the ground. The horse scrambled to his feet, leaving his rider prostrate on the ground.

Carol was off her mount in the twinkling of an eye. The other girls scrambled over or walked around the fallen tree which had caused the accident.

"Are you all right, Jan?" Carol asked anxiously.

Janet ruefully inspected herself. "I guess I'm all here," she acknowledged.

"I should have warned you about that tree," Ricky said. "You're really a good rider," she added.

"Of course, ow—oooo—ouch!" With mingled exclamations Janet managed to get to her feet with Carol's help. "And I wanted to show off!" she giggled. "How did the horse make out?"

"He is all right," Valerie said.

"We got our signals mixed," Janet continued laughingly. "He saw a green light and I a red one."

"How are we going to get the horses back over the fallen tree?" Carol asked. "I don't care to jump mine again."

"I'll jump them for you," Ricky said promptly.

The girls rode back to their instructor and the other girls. At the stables they dismounted again and watched while their horses were trotted away to their stalls.

In the sunset they limped toward their dormitories—Janet by far the most exhausted.

"I think I'll take a pillow the next time," she declared. "Then if the horse and I decide to separate I will have something soft to land on."

"The object is not to separate," Carol informed her. "Do you want to go riding tomorrow, Janet?"

"Riding!" Janet echoed distastefully. "I am not on speaking terms with my horse. No more riding for me this week! Tomorrow I shall go in for something gentle like baseball."

Carol laughed. "Baseball! You can't come within five feet of the ball with your bat."

"Woe is me," Janet said, gently depositing herself upon the dormitory steps. "Do I have to prove everything? Come to the athletic field tomorrow and I'll show you I can hit a home run."

Carol laughed derisively.

"I can, too," Janet insisted. "I hit you, don't I, when I throw a book at you?"

"Except when I duck and it goes through the window," reminded Carol.

"Don't sit there," Madge prodded Janet firmly. "We have to dress for dinner."

"And we have to get back to Happiness House," added Gale to Ricky and Gloria, but making no movement toward home.

"Isn't spring the most glorious time of the year," sighed Valerie. "When the grass is growing, the buds budding——"

"And the brooks brooking," Carol finished. "Come along," she urged Janet. "We have to dress and I'm hungry."

"I will be black and blue tomorrow," Janet prophesied gloomily. "My chagrin is mountainous. To think I had to fall off when we were going so good."

"Console yourself," Valerie soothed. "We shall probably all fall off sooner or later."

"I will live in hopes," Janet said brightly. "What are we going to do tonight?" she asked.

"I am going to study my history," Valerie said firmly. "Spring exams are just around the corner and I find my knowledge of dates strangely lax."

"Me for my geometry," Ricky said sorrowfully.

It developed that all the girls had more or less studying to do for the spring finals. Gradually they separated, Janet and Carol to drift upstairs to dress for dinner, Madge and Valerie to follow more leisurely. Gale walked to the sorority house with Ricky and Gloria. They separated only to meet again at dinner.

Afterward Gale went off alone to the solitude of her room to study. She would be glad to have Phyllis back with her again.

Chapter XVII

OMEGA CHI

May brought not only the round of festivities on May Day but the knowledge that they were in the last stages of the term. Freshmen were looking forward eagerly now to the time when they would be Sophomores. Seniors were looking forward with mingled joy and regret to the day when they would receive their diplomas.

One evening in May was always devoted to the sororities and clubs. It was then new members were chosen and new officers elected for the next term. The Omega Chi sorority always celebrated with a big party for their members. During the evening the newly elected members were sought out and informed of their good fortune in being selected to fill the vacancies left by Seniors going out.

The Omega Chi was eagerly sought by all the Freshmen. It meant not only belonging to the most popular group on the campus, but the girls were, for the most part, honor students, students likely to succeed in campus activities as well as their chosen profession later. There was no discrimination for the wealthy girls. The officers sought girls who were honorable, pleasant, and had a sense of humor. The standards they secretly set were sometimes hard to surpass and it was the reason the sorority had not a larger membership than it had.

On this night the officers of the Omega Chi were secreted in the dining room. Freshmen had been banished to their rooms. Other sorority members lounged about the living room or on the veranda outside. The tinkle of a guitar and the hum of girlish voices rose to Gale and Phyllis at the window of their room.

Phyllis had returned to the campus two weeks ago. As yet she had not been out of her room. That was something Gale could not understand. Doctor Elton had been so sure, so positive, that the first of May would see Phyllis as well as ever. Yet here she was still tied to her armchair at the window.

"A glorious night, Phyl," Gale said dreamily. "Did you ever see so many stars —or see them so close?"

"Listen to the girls singing," Phyllis said.

"'The girls of Omega Chi!'" The last words of the sorority song floated up to them.

"Do you suppose we would be fortunate enough to be elected to the sorority?" Gale asked.

Phyllis laughed. "If we aren't we will probably have to move next term."

"Perhaps I had better start packing," Gale laughed. "But seriously—I want terribly to get into Omega Chi. I like all the girls so much——"

"All the girls?" Phyllis asked lazily. "Even Marcia Marlette?"

"Don't spoil my evening!" Gale said quickly. "I refuse to think of her."

"You have to think of her," Phyllis laughed. "She might be president next term when Adele is no longer here."

"I hope not!" Gale said aghast. "The girls would never elect her—surely!"

"Funny things can happen," Phyllis reminded her.

"Phyllis——" Gale rested her chin on her hand and gazed at the moon. "Is your father coming to see you tomorrow?"

"Yes, why?"

"I've got something to ask him," Gale said. "Do you suppose Janet and Carol will get into the sorority?"

"What do you want to ask my Dad?" Phyllis interposed. "Is it—about me?"

"Yes," Gale said firmly, decisively. "He told me you would be hopping about like a sparrow by the first of May. You aren't and I want to know why," she said bluntly, watching Phyllis closely.

"I know," Phyllis said, bowing her head. "He told me too. He has done everything he can. It is my own fault that I'm not."

"What do you mean?"

"I'm afraid to try it," Phyllis said. "I'm afraid everything won't be as perfect as he says it will."

"But, Phyl, there is nothing to be afraid of——" Gale said gently. "It is all up to you now. You are only holding yourself back."

"I know," Phyllis said faintly. "But the day I came back to the campus—I tried to walk. The doctors and nurse made me get up and walk across the room—at least try to. I didn't make it. I fell and now—I'm afraid to try again."

"But that was natural for the first time," Gale soothed. "Darling, you've got to try it again."

"I'll try it when I get enough courage," Phyllis sighed. "But I'm running rather low on courage right now."

"But——" Gale began.

"Hist!" Ricky hissed from the door. "I have secret information that the new candidates have been selected," she informed them.

"Who are they?" Gale asked eagerly.

"Well," Ricky acknowledged, seating herself beside Gale, "that is still a mystery."

"They bring the girls from the other dormitory houses here, don't they, for the celebration?" Phyllis asked.

"Yes," Gale answered. "Look!" She pointed out the window. "There go two of the girls now—I'll wager they are going after some Freshmen."

The campus gradually became alive with girls, figures moving back and forth, each intent upon some errand. Suddenly two figures stepped out of the night below the girls' window. A few seconds later two more joined the first.

"Hi!"

They recognized Carol's gay voice and knew it was the remaining four Adventure Girls.

"Yes?" Gale called.

"We made it!" Carol shouted. "We're in!"

"And we are coming right up to see you," added Janet.

At the same moment a knock sounded on their door. An upper classman informed them that they, too, had been elected full-fledged members in the Omega Chi, and since one of their number was not able to come downstairs to partake in the reception for the Freshmen, they would bring the reception to their room. Gale's and Phyllis' room became the reception place for twenty new members. Adele, in her position of president, calmly took possession of Gale's desk over which to transact the business of her office.

The little group listened attentively to the purposes of the sorority as extolled by their president, and paid strict attention while the constitution and list of new officers were read to them. They were humorously reminded, before they broke up, that their initiation would take place at the beginning of the new term.

The next afternoon after classes Gale made her way to the lake. Doctor Elton had promised to have Phyllis there in the sunshine. Gale had made a flying visit to her room to don a bathing suit for a swim, and finding Phyllis absent, concluded that the Doctor had kept his word.

Gale had been thinking over what Phyllis told her last night. What a struggle had been going on in Phyllis' mind these past weeks and none of them had guessed! Just those few words on the night before had brought home to Gale the knowledge of what Phyllis was up against. The girl was afraid—terribly afraid that the miracle Doctor Elton had performed would not hold. Something must be done! The girls must do something to bring back Phyl's self-confidence. But what? Only Phyllis herself could really go through this trial. She must try her own strength. That was the only way she could ever possibly be sure of herself again.

Phyllis and her father were sitting on a bench overlooking the lake. Gale waved as they saw her approaching. Phyllis' hand was in the crook of her father's arm and she looked very happy. Gale told herself that the discovery of Phyl's father had worked miracles—all but the most important one.

Doctor Elton strolled away from Phyllis and approached Gale. Just out of earshot of the girl on the bench they stopped. They talked together for several minutes and then Gale came on to Phyllis while Doctor Elton went toward the campus.

"Glorious afternoon," Gale said dropping beside Phyllis.

"So nice and warm in the sunshine," Phyllis agreed. "Where did my Dad go?"

"Said he had a date with Doctor Norcot, but he will be right back. Have you seen Janet or Carol today?"

"No. Valerie told me they were riding again. Ricky flew away to join them when she heard of it."

"Been here long?"

"No. I waited for my Dad to bring me down," Phyllis said.

Gale looked at Phyllis, at the crutches lying on the grass at the side of the bench, and then away across the blue waters of the lake. Her eyes were narrowed in silent thought. She saw the thick growth of trees on the farther shore, the calm waters along the grassy bank almost at her feet, and the treacherous current farther out in the center of the lake, but it was not of these things she was thinking.

"Have you tried to walk today?" she asked.

"No."

"Why not?"

Phyllis sighed. "I'll try it some time—but now I'm too peaceful here."

"Doesn't your father want you to try?"

"That is all I hear," Phyllis said wearily. "He insists—and he is a great insister," she added smilingly.

"But you are just as determined to wait," Gale laughed. "Well, when you decide let me know." She stretched lazily. "I think I'll go for a swim."

From the pocket of her jacket she drew a red bathing cap and slipped it over her curls. She divested herself of her jacket and waved to Phyllis as she darted away.

"Don't go out too far and get caught in the current," Phyllis warned.

"I'll be all right," Gale called back.

Phyllis watched the blue waters close over her friend. With a little sigh she leaned back. She wished heartily she could be in there with Gale. However, she couldn't, so why worry about it?

Gale was having a glorious time. The water was cold but she did not mind it. Her strokes cut the water cleanly and swiftly. The water along the shore was calm and little ripples drifted up to the bank. Slowly and carefully Gale worked her way out a little farther, always mindful of the whirl of waters which swept continually to the falls at the farther end of the lake. Gale used to swim often in the waters of the bay near her home. She was an excellent swimmer and diver, one of the champions on the team at High School but she had not entered into the competition here at Briarhurst.

The sun was sinking farther into the west all the time and Phyllis was becoming impatient to get back to the sorority house, but she did want to wait for her father. Gale said he promised to return immediately, but so far he had not come. Gale was in the water a long time and Phyllis was thinking of calling her to suggest going back to Happiness House when she noted signs of distress from Gale. All was not well with her friend.

"Help, Phyl!"

Faintly Gale's voice came over the blue waters of the lake that separated them. Phyllis gripped the bench hard. Gale was struggling in the water to keep her head on the surface. Anxiously Phyllis looked about. The two girls were alone at this point. Phyllis called aloud but her voice echoed hollowly back to her. The frantic splashes in the water were becoming fainter as Gale grew weaker. Once again Phyllis shouted, but there was no answering call.

Gale was a good swimmer, she would pull through, Phyllis assured herself. But she was also reminded that even good swimmers had been known to drown —and Gale was being swept nearer and nearer to the swirling current. Phyllis uttered a swift silent prayer that help would miraculously come from somewhere —but it didn't.

The woods remained silent except for the little rustle of leaves and the twitter of birds. The water lapped the shore just as gently and undisturbedly.

Horror stricken, Phyllis saw Gale's red cap disappear beneath the surface. Anxiety, an urge stronger than herself to help Gale, gripped Phyllis. She forgot about the crutches lying on the grass, forgot that she was afraid to walk. Her eyes were on the water—seeking sight of the red cap. It bobbed to the surface and she rose to her feet. The cap disappeared beneath the blue waters again and Phyllis took several hasty steps toward the shore.

Miraculously her father appeared from a clump of shrubbery while from a little farther back in the growth of trees came Doctor Norcot.

"Oh—hurry—Gale——" Phyllis began desperately.

Doctor Elton let out a shrill whistle. Gale's red cap appeared on the surface and with clean-cut strokes the girl swam for the shore. She climbed dripping wet up the bank.

"Gale——" Phyllis began.

"Sorry to frighten you so, Phyl," Gale said lovingly, "but I didn't drown after all. Our plan worked, Doctor Elton," she added triumphantly.

"Your plan?" Phyllis murmured when for the first time she became aware that she was standing unassisted—she had actually walked alone for several paces!

Gale put a wet arm about Phyllis. "Darling, you did it!" she exclaimed. "You forgot yourself and walked."

"Then you weren't really in danger!" Phyllis echoed. "But I was so frightened I couldn't think of anything but——"

"Helping me," Gale finished. "That was exactly what we counted on."

Phyllis took a deep breath. "Now I'm going to walk back to the sorority house," she said determinedly.

Phyllis slipped her arm within her father's. With his help she led the way back to the campus. Doctor Norcot and Gale followed more slowly.

"Do you think she is doing too much at once?" Gale whispered.

"Doctor Elton knows best," the college physician replied.

Phyllis was in the most excellent of spirits when they reached Happiness House. She was tired but she would not admit it and insisted upon going down to the dining room for dinner to sit in her old place beside Gale. The girls greeted her with hilarity and a warm welcome. Even Marcia Marlette expressed her pleasure at seeing Phyllis back. But after dinner Phyllis went upstairs with Gale and immediately to bed. She was worn out not only with the unaccustomed physical activity but the mental strain.

Gale sat at the desk and wrote a long letter to Brent. Afterward she knelt at the window and let the May breeze ruffle her hair while she watched the lights in the other dormitories slowly being extinguished.

From the room upstairs came smothered giggles and a thump. Marcia Marlette and her roommate were having a party. Gale frowned at the night. Marcia, much to Gale's and the other girls' amazement, had been elected to the office of president of the sorority for the next term. How the feat had been accomplished Gale did not know, but she was not enthusiastic about it. Marcia could never be the friendly president that Adele Stevens had been this term. Gale rebuked herself. She mustn't believe the worst until it happened. Marcia had been exceedingly nice to Phyllis this afternoon. Perhaps the responsibilities of her new office would bring out the better side of Marcia's nature. But Gale doubted it. The next term did not look very bright for the sorority with Marcia at the helm of the organization.

Gale yawned and crawled into bed. The next term would have to take care of itself. Right now there was the question of whether Marcia and her friends would break through the ceiling.

Chapter XVIII

CAROL SLIDES

The balmy May afternoon saw the baseball game between the Freshmen and the Sophomores taking place on the athletic field behind Carver Hall. The players were most enthusiastic about this latest undertaking of theirs. It seemed most of the girls in the school had turned out to see this tussle between two feminine baseball teams and to hail the victor.

Janet, with supreme confidence in her own ability, had elected herself pitcher for the Freshmen. The girls had played several games and Janet had been pretty good, if not particularly brilliant. Carol, to support her pal, was catcher. Valerie was acting first baseman and Madge was shortstop. Their gymnastics teacher was the umpire and the Freshmen were sometimes suspicious of her friendly feeling toward the Sophomores. However, the nine Freshmen elected "Do or Die!" as their motto and went into the game with all the vigor and speed at their command.

But alas, the Sophomores were also good. They had experience added to their playing ability and for the first three innings scored four runs to the Freshmen's one. Janet, finding herself up against excellent batting ability, became nervous. Her throws to the home plate were a little wild and two girls walked to base.

Carol met Janet halfway between the pitcher's mound and the home plate where the next Sophomore stood swinging her bat.

"Are you good!" Carol scoffed. "I thought you were the world's wonder woman pitcher. I'm beginning to believe you are the world's worst."

"That's gratitude for you!" Janet sighed. "Here I nearly throw my arm out of joint and I get no credit from you."

"I told you to throw them a little low for Agnes and you didn't. You deliberately threw the ball at her bat. All she had to do was stand still and let it hit. It cost us another run."

"So what?" Janet said wearily.

"Come on, toots, do your stuff," Carol encouraged. "We've got to strike this girl out."

"Brackity saxe, saxe, saxe,
Brackity saxe, saxe, saxe,
Y-e-a, Freshmen!"

The spectators chanted loudly and enthusiastically. Gale and Phyllis led the Freshmen rooting section in an uproarious cheer. They yelled with all the abandon of children on a spree.

Janet beamed upon the crowd and swung the ball.

"St-uh-rike one!"

Carol ran out and handed the ball to Janet.

"Swell, pal!" she declared.

Janet beamed again and threw the ball.

"St-uh-rike two!" The Instructor was having as much fun out of the game as the girls were.

Janet, concentrating on the batter before her, had momentarily forgotten the girls on first and second base. The Sophomore on second base was an adventurous soul and now she took advantage of the pitcher's absorption to steal to third. Halfway there Janet saw her and threw the ball wildly to Madge, the short stop. The Sophomore dived for the base. The baseman received the ball from Madge while the Sophomore turned and dashed madly back toward second. The ball went again to Madge. The Sophomore tried once more for third base. The runner see-sawed back and forth until she was finally caught and pronounced out.

The Freshmen were jubilant, especially Janet and Carol. The pitcher returned to the work at hand and the batter-up was struck out.

The innings went on until the ninth. At that time the score stood twelve to ten in favor of the Sophomores. Janet had been relieved in the pitcher's position by another Freshman. However, in the last inning she returned.

Somehow the Freshmen managed to keep the score the same. They did not let the Sophomores score again and the side retired. The Freshmen were at bat.

"I don't like the wicked look in that pitcher's eye," Janet said as she stood beside Carol watching Valerie at bat.

"You probably won't hit the ball either," Carol pronounced sadly as Valerie struck out.

"Is that so?" Janet bristled with indignation. "Maybe I haven't made a home run this game yet but I've been waiting for a crucial moment."

"It looks like this is it," Carol laughed. "There goes another one of our girls—

out!" She sighed. "Ho, hum, we might as well give in. We need two runs, but we'll never make them with only one more girl—and you are it."

Janet frowned on her. "I'll hit that ball if it is the last thing I do!"

Carol's eyes twinkled as she watched Janet take her place before the catcher.

"She is angry," Madge commented.

"I tried to make her mad," Carol confessed. "When she is stirred up she plays much better."

"St-uh-rike one!"

Carol made a wry face at Janet. The latter frowned more viciously and gripped the bat securely in both hands. Carol nudged Madge significantly.

"She is really cross now."

The spectators were hushed. The game depended on Janet and what she did.

"St-uh-rike two!"

"Woe is me!" Carol murmured. "My psychology didn't work."

"She has one more chance," Madge said. "If she only gets on base and then someone else makes a run——"

"Two runs to tie the score! It might as well be ten," Carol said pessimistically.

"Look! Look!" Madge cried gleefully. "She did it! She socked that old ball way out——"

Janet had swung with all her strength and hit the ball squarely, sending it high into the air over second base. The Sophomore in her effort to get it overshot the mark and fumbled. Janet was away like a shot to first base, past first and safe on second!

"I hope I do as well," Carol remarked.

She was the next batter up. The Freshmen were still howling with delight over Janet's hit. The first was a foul ball. The second attempt Carol missed. But the third time! Like Janet, the necessity for action brought cool determination and steadied her. She hit the ball a resounding smack that sent it bounding along the third base line.

Janet was off to third base while Carol sped to first. Both girls were safe.

Now the game looked particularly bright for the Freshmen. With two girls on bases they had a good chance to even the score. But if one more was pronounced out the game was over and lost. Another Freshman stepped up to the home plate. She was nervous but determined.

Janet took several steps away from third base but kept a wary eye on the pitcher. She simply must get in and score! She looked at Carol.

Carol was edging away from the security of first base. The pitcher was looking at Carol. Janet went a little farther toward home. Carol suddenly dived toward second. The pitcher threw the ball to the second base. The baseman missed it and it bounded a few feet away. By the time the ball was secured Carol was safe on second base and Janet had stolen home.

The Freshmen fans were wild. They cheered lustily. Their team needed only one run to tie the score now!

The Sophomore pitcher seemed to have lost her grip on the situation. The Freshman at bat walked to first base. The next girl also walked. That forced Carol to third base. What a chance now to tie the score—even to win the game!

Carol watched the pitcher closely. She edged away from the base. The baseman followed. It all happened very suddenly. Carol in her exuberance and confidence in having stolen to second base once, thought she could do the same thing again. The pitcher was watching the strange motions of the girl at first base when Carol dived for the home plate. With lightning rapidity the pitcher whirled and tossed the ball. In a cloud of dust and cinders Carol slid into the catcher.

"Out!" the umpire said firmly, indisputably.

The Sophomores were jubilant, their team had won! The Freshmen were downcast, but they did their best to hide it.

"Of all the dizzy tricks——" Carol derided herself.

"You did great," Janet defended surprisingly. "We gave them a thrill anyway."

"But I had to spoil our big chance," Carol wailed. "If I had only waited——"

"What's the difference?" Valerie said gayly. "They only beat us by one point."

"And I hit the ball," Janet reminded her friend. "What did you say about my not being able to even see it?"

"I take it all back," Carol said humbly. Then she bristled with indignation. "I think I was safe at home, and I also think the umpire was on the Sophomores' side!"

"Tush!" Janet said. "Let's change and join Gale and Phyl."

For all of the other girls' levity Carol was inconsolable. She felt responsible for the girls losing the game and even though they in no way chided her or scolded she blamed herself.

"It was the best ball game I ever saw," Phyllis declared when they were all united on the East Campus Dormitory steps. "I never thought girls could play such good baseball."

"You have no idea what we can do," Janet told her condescendingly. "You should see us pull taffy."

"Whoops! How exciting," Madge laughed.

"Exciting or not, it is a good idea," Janet said. She beamed upon Gale and Phyllis. "If you two sorority sisters could find a way to come up and see us tonight we might have a taffy pull."

"We'll be there," Phyllis promised promptly. "Nothing could induce me to miss it."

"See you tonight then," Carol yawned. "I'm going to get some last minute studying in on my Geometry. Tomorrow is our final exam."

The other four girls disappeared within the dormitory house while Gale and Phyllis strolled toward Happiness House in the afternoon sunset.

"Let's go see White Star," Phyllis proposed. "We have plenty of time before dinner."

White Star was the mount in the stables which Phyllis had chosen for her own when she first started to ride two days before. She had long before visited the stables with the other girls and made friends with the black horse who had the white star on his forehead from which he got his name. She had ridden, too, that summer in Arizona but just two days ago had she begun her proper training at Briarhurst. Every day found her participating more and more in the activities which she had at first pursued when she came to college. Gale, too, did not need to act for Phyllis any more as president pro tem of the Freshman class. Phyllis was now able to attend to all the business in which she was involved.

There were no riding classes this afternoon and all the horses were in their stalls with only one groom on guard. White Star whinnied softly at the girls' approach. He was a magnificent animal—sturdy, and his satiny coat was smooth and shiny. He nuzzled Phyllis' shoulder with his soft nose.

"Get away, old softie," she said smiling. "Want some sugar?"

Eagerly the horse thrust his nose into her hand and secured the white lump.

"Do you carry a supply of sugar with you?" Gale laughed. "Every time you come here you have some and White Star knows it. He would follow you back to the sorority house if he could get out."

Phyllis rubbed White Star's forehead.

"He is a great horse," she said, "the only one I'll ride here at school." She brought forth another piece of sugar from her pocket. "That is the last!" she warned.

With a final pat for White Star the girls left the stall. The horse sent a soft whinny after them.

"The Dean is a lot more popular with the girls now than she was before, isn't she?" Phyllis murmured. "The new organ in the chapel, these riding lessons—everything has won the girls over."

It was true. The resentment against the Dean had miraculously faded with the realization that everything she planned was really for the benefit of the school and the girls there. All trouble had ceased with the departure of Miss Horton. Now Briarhurst was the most peaceful and harmonious spot in the world. But sometimes even the most blissful peace is rudely disturbed.

Chapter XIX

WHITE STAR

The taffy pull was most successful. With due secrecy Gale and Phyllis had managed to get out of Happiness House and into their friends' dormitory without being discovered. What really might happen if they were found would be serious but they were skylarking and they did not think of the consequences of their act. They were too intent on having a good time.

The high spot of the evening came when Carol's hands were both occupied with pulling the golden strands of sticky mass.

"Ooooo," she cried, "my ear itches. What'll I do?"

"Scratch it," Janet suggested practically.

"And get my golden curls all full of molasses?" Carol demanded. "Think of something else. Only hurry up—ooooooo!"

Valerie came to the rescue. She was the only one who had available a hand which was not entangled in the taffy.

After that they ate and pulled to their hearts' content. The evening flew away. When the lights-out bell rang Gale and Phyllis decided it was high time for them to be getting back to Happiness House. It would be quite a puzzle for them to get safely back to their room unseen. They hoped the door was not yet locked.

With the stealth of criminals they left the dormitory house. Once on the campus they paused in the shade of the trees to breathe freely. From a window Janet and Carol waved to their two friends and silently disappeared within the darkness of their room. The girls on the campus strolled leisurely toward the darkened Happiness House. They were really in no hurry and it was such a nice evening.

Some imp of mischief whispered in their ear and they turned toward the lake. They stood on the shore and watched the moonlight make little gold ripples on the waves. They explored the dark shadows of the thick growth of trees along the lake and shivered at the eerie noises.

Finally Gale became sleepy and they decided that they really must go back to their room. Tomorrow they had a difficult examination to pass, for which they had studied for days and days. It was important that they should be fresh in the morning.

"We really shouldn't have gone to that party tonight," Phyllis yawned. "I haven't a blessed Geometry thought in my head."

"We had fun though," Gale said. "I never ate so much taffy in my life."

"What would happen if we were caught in another dormitory house?" Phyllis wanted to know. "We wouldn't be expelled, would we?"

Gale made a wry face. "Why must you think of those things?"

Phyllis put a hand on Gale's arm. In the darkness of the trees they stood listening. They could hear the gentle lapping of the lake water almost at their feet. From over their head an eerie voice demanded:

"Who-o-o-o."

A pair of eyes glared down at them like green electric light bulbs suddenly flashed on and turned off then flashed on again as an owl blinked through the night.

"Doesn't he scare you?" Phyllis shivered. "He reminds me of a Hallowe'en goblin."

"We really should go to bed," Gale said once more, "as much as I hate to admit it."

"We've had a lot of fun this term, haven't we?" Phyllis sighed. "It is hard to believe that our Freshman year is almost over."

"Fun!" Gale echoed. "I wouldn't say you had so much fun," she added.

"On the whole I did," Phyllis declared, "and I even found a father! He is going to Marchton to see Miss Fields and move all my belongings," she continued.

"He is! What is going to happen to Miss Fields?" Gale asked.

"I asked him not to do anything about her," Phyllis said. "All I want is never to have to go back there."

"Then we won't see you much this summer," Gale sighed. "Marchton will seem different."

"Oh, I'll see you all right," Phyllis said but she did not explain further then.

The girls had left the wood shore line behind them and come out again upon the campus. Now they could see the stars above them twinklingly close.

"Look at that red glow back of the Chemistry Hall," Gale said suddenly. "What do you suppose it is?"

"I can't imagine," Phyllis said. "Something at the stables. Let's investigate."

Keeping in the shadows so as to be out of sight of any wandering teacher the girls crept around the Chemistry Hall. What they saw froze them momentarily to the spot with horror. Flames were curling around the corner of the main stable and smoke was pouring from a shattered window. From the groom's quarters stumbled one of the attendants. The other regular man was not on the grounds today.

"Gale," Phyllis said urgently, "there is a fire alarm attached to Carver Hall. Sound it! Tell the Dean——"

"Right!" Gale said promptly, not waiting to hear any more, and sped away.

Phyllis ran forward. "Are you all right?" she demanded of the man.

"The smoke——" he choked.

A frightened whinny from the stables brought Phyllis up short. The poor trapped horses! She couldn't stand there and do nothing!

"Get the fire apparatus working!" she shouted and dashed for the stables. Madly she dashed back again. "Got a knife?" she asked the groom.

Dazed from the smoke and the sudden confusion, where an hour ago had been peace, the man nodded his head and struggled to get a pen knife from his pocket. Once it was secured Phyllis dashed again to the nearest stall. The horses were trampling, rearing, whinnying in fright. The smoke was thick and it was impossible to breathe freely.

Phyllis was hurled against the side of the stall as the horse rose on his hind legs pawing the air wildly with his forehoofs, straining at the rope which tied his bridle to the stall. She picked herself up from the straw mumbling unintelligible things when she discovered she had dropped the knife. Her fingers found the rope but it was impossible under such conditions to untie the knot. Quite by accident, a lucky accident, her foot came in contact with the knife as she dodged another flying hoof. She picked it up and cut the rope. Pulling and coaxing she got the horse into the open air. She tied him securely to the hitching post where the girls were wont to dismount after their classes. It was a sufficient distance away from the burning stables to make him safe. It was absolutely necessary to tie him, although it wasted several precious minutes. Otherwise, with the queer trait of his breed, he would immediately have dashed back into the building.

Once more Phyllis returned to the stable. The groom had disappeared, probably in search of help and fire extinguishers. The uproar of the horses beat in her ears. Their frightened whinnies were even more pitiful than human cries might have been. The animals were so helpless! The second horse was led and tied to the post beside the first. She felt bruised where another flying forefoot had caught her off guard. The flames were roaring like a furnace now. The straw in the stables would be excellent food for the flames. Luckily the fire had started in the groom's quarter and must work up through the harness room. If it had started in the heart of the stables themselves she would never have been able to get near the horses.

One by one Phyllis brought the horses out. When the last one was secure she leaned weakly against the post. The alarm bell was tolling now. It had been ringing for several minutes but in her absorption she had not heard it. Soon the girls would be on the scene and the fire apparatus would be in play. Phyllis felt as if she would never again get the smell of smoke out of her system.

One—two—three—she counted the horses neighing and rearing at their posts. Nine! There should be ten! With a sinking of heart she looked at them all again. White Star was not there! White Star! The best of the group! How could she possibly have missed him?

Without another thought but that of her favorite mount Phyllis dashed back into the stables. One—two—three—stalls empty. Nothing but silence and the crackling of flames—flames creeping closer, destroying, and smoke.

Her head was whirling and she felt choked. Once she stumbled wildly over something and fell to her knees in the straw. She sat there several seconds, dazed. She had better find White Star soon or they would both be trapped! Why didn't help come? Though only a few minutes could have elapsed since she and Gale first sighted the fire it seemed like hours. What was that?

An excited whinny came to her, followed by the sound of crashing blows against wood. White Star! And he was trying to kick his stall to pieces! Despite the terribly desperate situation Phyllis could not help but smile. White Star proposed to fight! She stumbled to her feet and went on prowling through the smoke until she came to the stall in which all the uproar was taking place. She felt as though all the strength in her body was leaving her. White Star was bucking and kicking with all his might. The smoke was like a blanket smothering everything and through which Phyllis felt her way to White Star's head. She took hold of his bridle and he nuzzled against her shoulder affectionately. He seemed to recognize his friend. With her last remaining strength Phyllis cut the rope that held White Star. She turned him around and gave him a stinging blow.

"Go it, boy!"

The horse reared and plunged out through the door of his stall, leaving Phyllis a huddled figure on the straw.

Gale, after turning the electric switch that automatically sounded the fire alarm, had sped to the Dean's office. She found Dean Travis working late. After excitedly blurting out the news Gale dashed again to the stables, stopping for nothing. She was just in time to see White Star appear.

The horse bounded out of the smoke into the cool night air. He stopped short, raised his head and whinnied, pawing the ground with his forehoof. He glanced at the other horses, straining at their ropes, tossed his head, and turning, dashed back for the burning stable.

"Phyl——" Gale shouted.

There was no reply. Gale saw the groom and another man playing a stream of water upon the flames on one side of the building. She went closer. Through the smoke she could see White Star.

Gale could not explain White Star's actions. She had read of how horses always dashed back into the burning building from which they were rescued, unless they were tied outside. It was evident that Phyllis had tied the others, why not White Star? This was her favorite!

Gale looked at the other struggling horses and wondered at the strength of her friend. Horses were strong at any time—frightened, terrorized as they were now, she did not see how Phyllis had managed to get them all out.

White Star appeared out of the smoke and almost ran her down. He stood for a second looking at her, pawing the ground and tossing his head.

Gale remembered seeing a wonder horse in the movies who acted like this when he was summoning help for his master. Was it possible—— White Star was a magnificent animal. She had always acknowledged that, but she had never actually credited him with super intelligence. However, now his eyes seemed to be pleading with her; the crazy way he dashed about made her think he was trying to tell her something.

"Phyllis!" Gale shouted again.

"Ahoy." Carol and Janet dashed up breathlessly.

"We got here first because we didn't have to stop to dress seeing that we weren't yet undressed—if you understand me," Janet said.

"We might have known you would be here," added Carol. "Where's Phyl?"

"Look at that horse!"

The groom had taken it into his head to rescue White Star and tie him beside the other horses. But White Star had other ideas. He raced madly past the flames and into the smoke.

"I think I know what he wants!" Gale cried and the next time White Star dashed into sight she followed him.

"The crazy——" Carol began. "Gale, come back!"

Gale bumped into White Star. She was unable to see him clearly, the smoke hurt her eyes, and she was choking for breath. With one hand on his bridle she let him pull her along. The horse trotted forward until he came to his stall. There he stopped.

"W-What now?" Gale coughed. Dimly through the smoke she became aware of a figure lying on the ground. "Phyl!" she screamed. "Phyl!"

A burning rafter crashed to the ground at some little distance. White Star reared and plunged away but a second later he was back, trembling and whinnying. Gale lifted Phyllis and put her across White Star's back. Necessity and fear had lent her strength and now she pulled White Star's head down to her shoulder. With a tight grip on his bridle she started forward at a run. The horse plunged after her. How she managed to dash out through the smoke Gale didn't quite know but thankfully she had come at last to her friend.

Chapter XX

THE END OF THE TERM

"I am personally going to buy White Star a whole box of sugar for his very own," Carol said positively. "The horse is a hero."

"And he speaks a language all his own," added Janet. "Gale understood him but we didn't."

"It is lucky for me that Gale did understand him," Phyllis said lazily.

It was the last day of classes, weeks after the fire at the stables. The girls were gathered on the campus after their last classroom session, discussing the high points of their college term. The miraculous way White Star had summoned help for Phyllis never ceased to be a thing of wonder to them. Neither Phyllis nor Gale had suffered other than a slight sickness from smoke. New stables had been erected and riding classes had gone on as before, with the exception of White Star's sensational rise in popularity.

"All the girls want to ride him," Madge laughed, "but he seems to prefer Phyllis."

"Ah, yes, brothers under the skin," Carol giggled daringly. "What is this power you have over horses, Phyl?"

"The same you have over Chemistry professors," Phyllis retorted. "What I want to know is, why did Professor Lukens pass you?"

"Because I'm brilliant," Carol said modestly.

"More likely because he wanted to be rid of you," Janet put in. "You asked more questions in class than——"

"Let's go down to the village and get a soda at the drug store," Madge proposed peacefully.

"An excellent suggestion," Carol said immediately. "Why don't you think of things like that?" she asked Janet.

"Because walking doesn't appeal to me," Janet said promptly. "Now if—behold!" she said in astonishment.

The girls were at the edge of the college grounds. Mounting the hill to the gate was a new, shiny bus which declared in broad white letters on the side "Briarhurst College." At the wheel was the same old fellow who had met them in his dilapidated contraption when they arrived at Briarhurst and who had been so against the new Dean because she wanted to buy him a new bus.

"Say, did somebody leave you money?" Janet shouted.

He stopped the bus and opened the door. "Want a ride to the village? Ain't she a beauty?" he asked next when the girls had accepted his invitation with alacrity and tumbled into the vehicle. "The new Dean's responsible. Course," he added condescendingly, "she ain't as good as old Lizzie but she's sure spiffy!"

Janet and Carol chortled with glee.

"Spiffy is exactly the word!" Carol declared.

At the foot of the hill he let them out and went on his way.

"Miracle number two," Carol laughed. "Remember how fond of his old bus he was?"

"Now he is even more proud of this one," Madge agreed.

"Lead me to the drug store," Janet said firmly.

"What are we going to do this summer?" Valerie asked over her chocolate soda.

"Let's go camping," Madge proposed. "We can have a lot of adventures that way."

"Hm," Janet agreed unenthusiastically.

"My dad," Phyllis said slowly, "has offered to let us use his boat—if we want to."

"If we want to," Janet echoed gleefully.

"Carol Carter! Did you suggest it to Doctor Elton?" Gale asked, trying to be stern but failing.

"Well," Carol murmured, "it might have slipped out in my conversation with him. You see I——"

"We see," Valerie laughed.

Suppose we leave the Adventure Girls here, discussing their plans for the summer. We shall join them again for more excitement in The Adventure Girls on Vacation.

End

CPSIA information can be obtained
at www.ICGtesting.com
Printed in the USA
BVHW031534020120
568385BV00001B/113/P

9 781679 559358